About the Author

Asher Drapkin has been interested in writing Sci-Fi and fantasy since taking an interest in Astronomy from age five. He has been a member of Leeds Astronomical Society and Leeds Writers' Circle. He started his working life, age fifteen, as an apprentice watchmaker. During his military service he was an aircraft instrument technician in the Royal Air Force. Besides writing he enjoys gardening, and occasionally bread making.

An avid reader he likes H.G Wells, Isaac Asimov and Ray Bradbury.

His other interests include, Philosophy and language.

Dedication

Many thanks to my 'Mentor' Mandy Sutter, writer and poet who conducted creative writing sessions.

For the Staff at Leeds General Infirmary.

Thanks to advice given by members of Leeds Writers' Circle, and the Writers who lead the sessions at Leeds Trinity University's Writing Festivals.

Also a thank you to my friends Cantor David Apfel, Ivan Green and Louis Buton for their interest.

A big thank you to my sponsor 'madebynaomi.co.uk' (Handmade Jewellery and greetings cards.

Not forgetting Vinh and the Staff at Austin Macauley.

Asher Drapkin

BEST SELLER WRITER

AUSTIN MACAULEY PUBLISHERS™

LONDON • CAMBRIDGE • NEW YORK • SHARJAH

A CIP catalogue record for this title is available from the British Library.

ISBN 9781787108318 (Paperback)
ISBN 9781787108325 (E-Book)
www.austinmacauley.com

First Published (2018)
Austin Macauley Publishers Ltd.
25 Canada Square
Canary Wharf
London
E14 5LQ

Acknowledgements

I must make special mention of the fact that my wife, Myra's understanding that the time I spend on the computer writing is my enjoyment even though household matters have fallen on her shoulders.

Chapter One

"I've arranged for us to go out to dinner with Ann and Harold."

"You know I detest the bloke—I do wish you'd consulted me first."

The trouble with my wife is that although she means well and has my best interests at heart, she always 'goes off half-cocked' as the saying goes.

"Considering I've been on the horns of a dilemma, deciding which of my new dresses to wear, you could at least be more accommodating. You know, Ann and I have been friends since college. When was the last time you took me out? Bet you can't remember."

As always in such a situation, I changed my mind.

"Okay, very well, we'll go. I just hope Harold does not provoke any argument with me."

"Perhaps you shouldn't take the bait. Just ignore it and raise another topic. Better still, say something to Ann. You know she likes you."

"I suppose you're right. I can't understand why Harold always resents other people's successes. It's not as though he's short of a bob or two. His antique business is doing well and he drives a big car. I, on the other hand, can't drive and have to rely on others if I want to go anywhere."

"As I say, just play it cool. We are going to your favourite restaurant 'Only the Best'. No doubt you'll run into other writers that you know. I'll bet some were at your book launch.

I must say I never thought that so many people would be interested."

I couldn't help but put on a wry smile. "That, my darling, is because you do not appreciate science fiction or fantasy. Although, as I said in the foreword, maybe it is all true. That is what the fascination of the book is. And furthermore, my agent phoned me late last night because, not only are television producers interested, we've had enquiries from Hollywood. I think I'll mention that at dinner just to upset Harold."

"I suppose I should be thankful that you've agreed to go. I do wish though that you wouldn't go out of your way to upset Harold."

"I can't be held responsible if the world adores and appreciates my creative writing. I'm afraid Harold will just have to live with it. Remember the old saying 'it's tough at the top'?"

"Very well. In the meantime, help me choose which dress to wear."

"Do I have to?"

"There are only two to choose from. I'm sure you can manage that."

With deep reluctance, I followed Sandra up to the bedroom. On her bed lay the two dresses, both of which would've suited her.

"So what do you think?"

"The one that has the various sizes of rectangular patterns."

"So, what's wrong with the other one?"

I anticipated the question, so I had a prepared answer. I knew the response would be aggressive in tone, so I made sure my response would be long and drawn out.

"Although I like both, the aesthetic side of my nature is drawn to the one I prefer because the colours and rectangular shapes are quietly subdued and, at the same time, exciting artistically. The other one, even though it carries my favourite colours, I feel it is somewhat loud and aggressive and, to a certain extent, distracts from the lady who wears it. In other words, it gives the impression that it is a work of art rather than an article of clothing."

"I might have known you'd say something daft. I don't know why I bother asking you."

That was the sort of comment I thought she would make.

"Tell you what, I'll select my outfit for this evening. Oh, and just bear in mind, I'll wear whatever I choose, irrespective of your opinion." I was determined not to be told what I could or could not wear.

Before she could answer, I continued, "How are we getting there? Are you taking our car or what?"

"No, we agreed that we'd go in their new car, which is bigger and roomier than ours."

"Thank goodness for that. This means Harold can feed his ego, which means I can sit back and ignore him."

"Maybe if you tried a little harder to be more sympathetic towards him, he would respond in kind. Don't forget, he didn't have an easy time growing up in the war years."

"Are you saying I did have an easy time? He's only a few months older than me, and he did not have to be called up for National Services like me. This meant he was earning a real wage whilst I had to cope with a Serviceman pay. What I mean is a National Serviceman's pay. So, who had the easy start in life? Him or me?"

With that, I entered my computer room/ other bedroom and proceeded to dress. Although I wanted to wear a bowtie, I decided not to because that would be too much of a challenge to miss. So, blazer with RAF badge, white shirt, RAF tie and navy trousers were my selection. Must admit that was the get-up I always wear when going out with Harold and Angela. It is my way of subtly (or maybe not so subtly) reminding Harold that I served in Her Majesty's Forces whereas he did not. I called out to Sandra, "I'm dressed and ready to go. I'll wait outside."

"Okay, I'll be as quick as I can."

I was tempted to make a comment but decided not to. Instead, I stepped out into the driveway and had a good look at the back garden. The hosta leaves were turning yellow, the lone pink hollyhock was now taller than the garage, and the hydrangeas almost covered the back fence.

"What a pity!" I thought that my work and writing schedules do not give me time to appreciate the beauty of my gardens. After all, it was due to my efforts that it thrives and blossoms. Almost immediately, a large 4 × 4 drew up, followed by a toot on the horn. I called out to Sandra, who had just made her way downstairs.

"This must be the new car Ann spoke about. It looks quite roomy from the outside."

I was not particularly impressed. Basically, I'm a spiritual person and, quite frankly, detest any form of materialism. I've always maintained that such an attitude is a disease that evokes jealousy. As far as I'm concerned, a car is an object that makes it convenient to go from place to place.

"I'm really looking forward to tonight's meal. Haven't had much to eat all day," said Ann who, as always, looked and sounded ravishing. Sandra knows Ann likes me. What I hope she does not know is that I like her very much. In fact, if I thought I could get away with it, I'd have no qualms about 'hitting on her', as they say in America.

The car pulled away with ease, engine sounding like a dull, purring cat. I asked Harold how long he'd had the new car. He retorted for long enough. His tone was sharpish that suggested resentment at my question. I thought to myself, if he wants to be like that all evening, then I'll engage Ann in conversation and put on the charm, even though Sandra may not like the idea. After all, I had learned some years ago from an old friend that life being so short, one should try and enjoy every moment.

"So Ann, how's life treating you? What do you think of the new car? Antiques must be doing well."

Sandra gave me a dig in the ribs. She quickly blurted out that she and Ann had decided that there would be no talking about writing or antiques. And that all subjects must be positively neutral. Not wanting to provoke any argument, I just sat back and enjoyed the ever-changing scenery on the way to the restaurant. Ann asked why I had insisted on going to this restaurant.

"I come here about once a month with the Writing club, of which I'm the chairman. And considering most of the members are female and they like it, I naturally had no alternative but to acquiesce to their choice. I must say, it is a good choice, not just because of the food on offer, but there are several rooms to choose from. When the club meets, we book the Rose Room because it has good seating for writers and the tables are just the right height." By this time, we arrived at our destination and Harold had no difficulty finding a place to park. The car itself was fitted with an automatic parking-spot finder.

"So, where do think is the best room for our meal, Donald?" Ann's tone was what you would call mildly sexy. I took her lead by oozing charm and said that I would leave it up to her and Sandra. I knew it would take them at least five to ten minutes to decide, which would give me time to enjoy the cool night air. Harold, however, was being his usual impatient-self.

"I, for one, am not going to waste my eating time. I've had a hard day and I am hungry." With that, he turned on his heels, went barging through the main doors, ignored the 'Please Wait

Here' sign and sat down at the table right in the centre of the room. I knew for a fact that Sandra would never dream of sitting at a centre table. From where I was standing outside, I could see Ann and Sandra leaving the ladies room.

I decided that I would not get involved in the argument that was bound to ensue. So, gliding my way between the decorative trees, I managed to sneak in and head for the men's room. Once inside, I splashed water over my face, combed my hair, and with a dead, nonchalant expression, headed to the table. As expected, an argument was in progress.

Not just between Harold and our respective wives, but also a waiter who was trying to explain that the table was reserved for another party. When Harold protested that there was no sign on the table indicating it was reserved, I decided it was my turn to intervene.

"What is going on here then?" I made sure that my voice was comical. Naturally, I knew what was happening, so I made an interjection above the irate crosstalk.

"When my writers club meets here, we always sit in the Rose Room, which is comfortable. By any chance, is there a table free there now?"

"I'll find out, sir," replied the waiter.

It was not long before he returned.

"Yes, sir, you may choose any place you like. By the way, sir, are you by any chance Don Donaldson whose book 'The Dilemmas' has just reached the bestseller list?"

I confirmed his observation. He then asked me if I would sign his copy of the book and would I be contemplating a sequel? The truth is, I always like to finish my stories in a way that will draw the reader into a follow-up. Rather than dealing with our meal requirements, he went on to talk about books and writing in general. Harold, by now, was working up a lather.

"Excuse me, but I thought this place was a restaurant that served food and not a meeting place for idle chatting."

By the time he'd finished speaking, the other diners had stopped eating and turned their heads in our direction. His voice had reached a crescendo. The head waiter approached us.

"Is there a problem here?" his voice calm but deep and booming. Harold let rip saying he had been waiting for more than twenty minutes and nobody had taken his order. The head waiter then castigated the subordinate waiter and in a brusque manner, demanded that he take Harold's order. Irrespective of who was right or wrong, I thought it was bad form to shame the waiter publicly. I got up, headed for the manager's office, where his secretary was seated in her usual place, to the right of the entrance door.

"Evening, Margaret, is Mr Charles at home?" I asked with a grin.

"I'm okay, Mr Donaldson, and yourself?"

"I'm rather annoyed with your head waiter. He has just castigated one of his staff in front of all the diners in the Rose Room."

"What happened, exactly?"

I explained the details of the incident, emphasising that Harold was also out-of-order.

"I'll just check that Mr Charles is available. I know he has been up to his neck in it all day. Oh, by the way, can you confirm the date of your group's next meeting?"

It was lucky that I always kept a small pocket diary on me. "Next Thursday—will that be okay? The usual table layout. I'm expecting a bigger turnout than usual."

She assured me there would be no problem and if we required a meal, it would help if I could let her know in advance. I said I'd do my best. Margaret then buzzed the manager, who responded immediately. After explaining about

15

my complaint, he asked her to take full details and that he would look into the matter later.

"Well, what happened?" Sandra asked. She sounded irritable. This was a sign that a full-blown argument was about to ensue. I told her that my complaint would be looked into as soon as possible.

"Are you ready to order, sir?' I looked up and a very charming young girl—possibly in her early twenties, smiling sweetly, pencil and pad at the ready.

"What is the soup of the day?" I asked in a demure tone.

"Cream of tomato."

"Well, in that case, I'll start with the soup, followed by fish and chips." My choice did not meet with Sandra's approval.

"You are not going to eat fish and chips in a posh place like this."

I replied that if she thought that fish and chips were plebe food, why on earth would they serve it?

"By the way, I always order fish and chips when I eat here with the writing club. They know my tastes and they prepare it just how I like it."

Before she could think of a comment, I suggested that if she is feeling snobbish, I would recommend grilled salmon with chips. Must admit, I enjoyed Ann's smile and laugh.

"He got you there, Sandra."

I was beginning to enjoy this encounter. Sandra was only too well aware that Ann liked me a lot, so anything that would put me in a good light was bound to irritate Sandra. I took the opportunity to stoke up the fire.

"You'll have to forgive Sandra, she doesn't get out much in the real world, poor thing. That's why all her views on life are just one cliché after another. Now, for people like you and me, Ann, the worldly ones, creative thoughts are always at the forefront of our minds."

Sandra, gritting her teeth, gave me one of her usual 'I'm exasperated' looks.

For the next ten minutes or so, we all concentrated on our meals. The only chit-chat was 'How's yours?' followed by fine and 'what about yours?' 'also fine'. The next item that evoked a discussion was when the wine waiter asked if we would like something to drink. As always, when eating fish and chips, I asked for a Sauterne Bar sac. This prompted Sandra to exclaim, "You are not having wine with fish and chips. How utterly revolting!"

I responded, be that as it may, that's how I enjoy it. Furthermore, I asked her, trying not to sound sarcastic, since when did she become a wine buff? By this time, Sandra was becoming agitated. Through gritted teeth, she managed to rasp out that it would be so nice, if for just once, we could go out to dinner without letting remarks develop into a full-scale argument. Ann looked across at me, smiled and waved her forefinger in a derisory fashion. I responded by saying that basically, I was not, in any way, the argumentative type. I continued, "So it must be one of you three, if not all of you, who are basically confrontational."

Before either of them could say anything, the head waiter came bursting in. He threw his jacket on the floor, undid his bowtie and sent it flying across the room. All the diners stopped eating. He blurted out, "Let's see if Mr Charles can find anyone who is only half as good as me. No chance! Definitely, absolutely not!"

With that, he left towards the staff cloakroom, still shouting louder and louder that Mr Charles was a fool and an idiot. Out of the corner of my eye, I noticed Margaret coming into the dining area. I called out to her, "Trouble at the mill, Margaret?"

"I'll say, that man is a fool to himself. After you left and I spoke to Mr Charles about your complaint, he called him in and asked him to apologise to Henry, the waiter who was serving you. He refused point-blank because—to quote his own words: 'I'm in the right. You don't keep a customer waiting.'"

"So, then what happened?" I asked.

"Mr Charles said that he had asked him nicely to apologise and then went on to say: 'Now I'm giving you an order. Apologise to Henry.' He refused to comply."

"Then, refusing to do as he was told by his boss comes under the heading of Industrial Misconduct," I added.

"You are right. Mr Charles asked me to make out a cheque for a month's salary in lieu of notice."

"Bet you enjoy your feeling of power, Donald. You've got somebody the sack. You must be right proud of yourself."

"Excuse me, Harold—did you not hear what—?"

Before I could finish speaking, three members of the writing club came over to me. They asked me, laughing and smiling, how it felt being a celebrity. The fact that by any standards, they could only be described as very beautiful women, must have annoyed Harold even more, especially as one of them gave me a right passionate kiss. Sandra's eyes widened as she sat back, either shocked or surprised. Quickly, I introduced them to Sandra, whom I described as 'the light of my life'.

They explained that they were here celebrating one of their husbands' birthday. Eventually, they returned to their table. As they were leaving, I turned to Sandra and said, "It takes some getting used to being a celebrity. I do hope I'll be able to cope. It must be true what they say, 'It's tough at the top'."

Out of the corner of my eye, I saw Harold fuming, although he was trying to be calm and nonchalant. Perhaps I was feeling rather wicked, but I could not help but enjoy his discomfiture. I was just about to continue eating when Harold, somewhat surreptitiously, leaned back in his chair and pulled out his mobile.

After a moment or two, he said in a loud voice, "It's a bit awkward, I'm having dinner with my wife and friends."

Then after a longish pause, he continued, "If that's the case, I'll drive over. Should be with you in about twenty minutes. Thanks for letting me know."

Sitting forward, he exclaimed, "Must leave you folks. A business opportunity has come my way, so I must dash."

Ann looked crestfallen. "Do you really have to go now? You've hardly touched your dinner."

"I'll have something later at home. I can drop you off if you leave with me. I'm sure Don won't mind picking up the bill. After all, now that he is a celebrity, I'm sure he can afford it."

I decided not rise to his bait. I just said, "No problem. After all, business is business. If my agent were to call me now with an important offer, I too, would have to leave."

I suspected that Harold had just picked up his mobile and had a fake conversation with himself just so he could leave. Perhaps, I was being somewhat cynical. I had no way of finding out. The bottom line was, he and Ann left. I reminded her that I might be a little late for my talk with her group. As soon as they were out of earshot, Sandra asked how we would be getting home.

I replied, "You see that lovely lady over there who gave me that most enjoyable passionate kiss? She lives not far from us. Oh, and by the way, the man sitting opposite her, the one you keep staring at, is her husband."

"I have not been staring at him at all. I don't know why you come out with such rubbish."

Her tone sounded like indignation. I was teasing her but I wanted to see just how long she would protest her innocence.

"Tell you what, let's go over to their table and ask for a lift. I'll introduce you to him."

Sandra's reaction went off the indignant scale.

"We'll do no such thing. The very idea!"

I was feeling good but also mischievous.

"Come on, you know you are dying to meet him. Let's face it, all women adore Clive. No need to feel embarrassed. You should see how all the women at the gym ogle him."

By this time, Sandra was getting angry.

"The joke is over, Donald. Give it a rest."

I think the wine must have gone right to my head. I called out to Clive: "My wife thinks you are right dishy and would like to meet you."

Sandra rose from her chair, threw her napkin on the table and with fiery daggers in her eyes said, "Right, that's it! I'll make my own way home. You are an absolute swine!"

I could see that she was determined to leave, so I got up, dashing over to her just as she was about to take her first step. "Steady on, Sandra, can't you take a joke? Come on, let's have a word with Clive."

I took hold of her firmly but ever so gently and, despite her struggling to hold back, we reached Clive's table.

"Good evening, Clive. May I introduce you to my very lovely wife, Sandra. She's been dying to meet you."

"A pleasure to know you, Sandra. Has Don been misbehaving? It's nothing new. You should see how he carries on with ladies at the gym."

Sandra smiled gently. Clive went on to say that he didn't think I deserved Sandra to be my wife. This had the effect of calming Sandra down. After asking Clive if he would mind giving us a lift home, he suggested that we should have coffee at his and Joan's place. We agreed and soon we were enjoying not only coffee, but cheese and biscuits as well. We ended up staying with them for over an hour.

Clive did his best to comfort Sandra. He said that I should compensate her for the way I treated her at the restaurant. When Sandra complimented them on the nest of tables, Clive, who has a woodworking furniture business asked if we had a nest of tables. Sandra said no, but had been nagging me to buy one. Ever the businessman who never missed a chance to make a deal, Clive said that in view of the way I had behaved towards her, I should buy a nest, which he would supply at a reasonable cost.

I'm pleased to say Joan came to my defence.

"Poor Don. Just because he was having a joke, everyone is having a go at him. Come, sit next to me, Don. As a fellow writer, I understand the pressures we have to endure, especially when you have just entered the Bestseller list."

Clive gave Joan a wry smile.

"I know you writers always stick together. Have you ever considered what it is like for the partners who must endure your temperamental moods? Don't you agree, Sandra?"

Sandra nodded in agreement, but then added that, most of the time, I was in the library. There, I build up my writer's mood, and by the time I return home, I'm ready to upset the atmosphere. Clive commented that I do not deserve Sandra as a wife. He extended her his deepest sympathy.

Arrangements were then made for Clive to visit us the following day with his catalogues. Sandra looked pleased and said she was looking forward to it. I then thought that my leg pulling at the restaurant had hurt her deeply. I wondered perhaps whether there could be domestic storms ahead. I was thinking just how I could make amends, when Joan leaned over to me and kissed me on the cheek.

"Don't let that nasty couple over there upset you. I know that not only are you a good writer, you are also a good person who loves his wife very much."

After laughter all round and a few more minutes of general chit-chat, Joan said she would give us a lift home. As we made for the door, Clive and Sandra kissed and hugged. Sandra said she was looking forward to seeing him. She gave me a smile. Back home, I tried thinking how I could end hostilities between us. Usually, an offer to make a cup of coffee did the trick. So, as I could not think of anything better, I said, "How about a coffee? I'm making one for myself. It'll be no trouble."

"Oh, what a pity! If it would be a trouble for you then I would have said yes. As it is, I prefer nothing from someone who embarrassed me in public. In any case, I'm tired and want to go to bed."

With that, she spun around and walked off, still in an angry mood. For once, I found myself in a 'don't-know-what-to-do situation'. I kept asking myself, *was my teasing all that bad?* Perhaps it might have been. I don't think it was. It is not as though Sandra does not have a sense of humour. Must have been something else as well. So, mulling the evening's events over, as I was preparing my coffee, it occurred to me that she could have still been smarting over the argument with Harold. So, now what? Do I try and patch things up now or wait till morning? Either way, I'll still be in the doghouse. Finally, I took my drink to the lounge, switched on the TV and watched an old comedy film.

The following morning, I woke at around six. Sandra was gently snoring, which meant that in an hour or so, she'd be slowly making her way to the bathroom. Quickly, I washed and dressed. Went downstairs to the kitchen and as per our regular routine, opened the fridge and took out a bottle of chilled orange juice. Then, two slices of toast topped with soft, white cheese were the openings for today's breakfast. Meanwhile, the coffee percolator was set in motion.

This gave me time to work out my strategy that would help diffuse the upcoming battle with Sandra. There would be lots of work at the office and a potential new client to discuss matters with, due an hour or so before lunch. So, a clear head and a happy disposition were essential. After much thought, which in the end only produced a series of dilemmas, I decided that I would behave as though nothing had happened. In that way, Sandra would have to work out the best way to punish me.

Just as I was finishing my coffee, the kitchen door opened.

"There's still some coffee in the percolator if you want."

"Does that make you believe that it's your idea of an apology?"

Her tone was even and calm, with just a touch of anger. This gave me a clue as to how I should respond.

"No, Sandra. I was thinking that by way of an apology, I could take you out at the Martins, the—"

"And just how would that make me patch things up with Harold and Ann? I don't think I'll ever be able to go there again. The only true friend I've ever had, and you had to ruin everything by embarrassing me just because you didn't listen to me when Harold said what he did."

"Be that as it may. Tell you what, I'll phone Ann. I need to speak to her about my talk with her group. I'm sure I'll be able to patch things up. Maybe I won't be welcome there, but that doesn't mean that you won't be."

For a few seconds, Sandra seemed to be taken off-guard. I felt that she was thinking hard about something disapproving. I was not wrong.

"You do say some daft things. How could I possibly go there on my own every time I would like to see her?"

By now, time was moving on, so I had to think of something fast.

"Tell you what. Let's invite them here, one day next week for dinner and afterwards, watch something on TV."

"And do you think Harold would feel comfortable coming here? I doubt it."

"Okay—you phone Ann, explain my suggestion and see what she says about Harold. After all, I'm not the sort of person who holds on to a grudge. Come to think of it, despite Harold's many faults, I'm sure he too doesn't hold on to a grudge."

"Well, okay, we'll see what happens. Oh, and by the way, you will still have to take me out to the Martins."

I breathed a sigh of relief and looked at my watch.

"Must dash! I have an important meeting with a new client. See you later?"

I had just got out of my chair when my mobile came to life.

"Hello, Jackie, what's new? Really? Right, I'm on my way to the office, so you can fill me in later. Cheers!"

I turned to Sandra.

"That was my new agent. They told me she was a sharp one. Anyway, guess what? Hollywood might be interested in making a film based on my book. She'll let me know later."

"That's good for you. Better get on your way. I have a lot to do making the house presentable for Clive. He will be here at about eleven and I want to look my best."

I was taken aback at her looking good for Clive. Sandra must have read my mind.

"After all, he is really dishy, as you pointed out to me in the restaurant. Couldn't help but notice his deep chocolate eyes and those magnificent shoulders. I can see why the ladies at the gym go for him."

"I should join the gym. Then he could admire my fulsome figure."

I wasn't sure whether she was kidding just to get back at me for the restaurant incident. On the other hand, because I spend so much time at the office or writing, she might be tempted to have an affair.

"If you don't shift, you'll miss the bus. Go on, get on your way."

After running to catch the bus and sitting down breathless, I looked out of the window and mulled over what just had happened at breakfast. The sad conclusion was that it was my own stupid fault. If only I had not argued with Harold. Thus, I must fork out for a nest of tables, pay an arm and a leg for an expensive dinner at the Martins, and what if Sandra had made her mind up to have something on the side with Clive?

By the time I arrived at the office, I was feeling out of sorts. Not the sort of state to be in when dealing with a new client. Only one thing for it. I headed straight for the washroom, turned the cold tap full-on, kept my head down for about ten seconds, then snorting and spitting, followed by a rough rub-down with the towel and I felt a little better. So, with a great effort focused on the new account, I picked up the file and turned over a few papers. I had just underlined a few salient points that I thought could be useful, when my mobile played. It's someone's calling tune. It was Jackie.

"Yes, Jackie, it's okay, what's the gen?"

I took down all the details. No doubt about it, this agent was at the top of her game. I said I would have to speak to Sandra before I could go ahead. Jackie insisted that I call her back in twenty minutes, no later. As she put it, she has no time for time-wasters. I lost no time in calling Sandra. "Sandra, I've some good news and some not-so-good news. Jackie called me. Hollywood is interested in my book. So much so that there could be an eleven-million-dollar contract in the offering. It all depends on the results of a whirlwind book signing, events starting in New York, then Chicago and, after that, all over the place. If the publicity tops, then it's off to Hollywood to sign the contract."

"That's terrific, Don! Well done! So, what's the bad news?"

"The bad news is, I told Jackie that I wouldn't go without you. She said the agency couldn't afford to pay for you as well."

Sandra's comment threw me, "You big dope! Of course, you should go on your own. It's only a business trip with eleven million dollars for us at the end. Besides, with you out of the way, my dishy Clive and I could enjoy ourselves better."

My only thought was that she is making me suffer. Talk about a dilemma. If I don't go, then Jackie would, no doubt, refuse to include me in her list of authors. If I do go, I'll be wondering all the time whether Sandra is kidding or having an affair. But, how could I turn down the chance of becoming a millionaire? In the end, I decided I must focus on the money.

"If you are sure that you don't mind me going off on my own, then I'll tell Jackie that it is okay. I am right in thinking that you were just teasing me about you and Clive."

"That's for me to know and you to worry about. Besides, how do I know you won't throw yourself at some Hollywood starlet?"

"Now, come on, Sandra. You are the only one for me and I am a man of principle."

"Oh really, you know the old saying—'when the cat's away, he will play.'"

Finally, we both ended up laughing. She continued, "Please go and bring back eleven million dollars, which I'll enjoy spending. In the meantime, I'll have some fun with Clive." With that she said goodbye.

The intercom buzzer interrupted my train of thought. "George Smith is here, Mr Donaldson."

"Good. Show him in and serve him coffee and biscuits as well."

"Pleased to meet you, Mr Smith. Take a seat."

"Call me George and would you please sign this copy of your book? My wife bought a copy yesterday and she wouldn't let me out of the house if I didn't get the book autographed."

"I can see your wife is a good, discerning reader. What is her name?"

"Paula".

"I'll write something special for her."

I wrote: "To Paula, hope you enjoy reading this book. I am not sure whether there will be a sequel or not, although I have a few ideas for another story, which I hope you will buy. Regards, Don Donaldson."

I handed the book back and we proceeded to talk business. After explaining exactly the type of engineering products his factory made, I could come up with several suggestions of magazines where we could pitch the products.

When I pointed out several foreign periodicals, he became quite enthusiastic because the export market would be something new. It took a little longer negotiating our costs but finally, just before lunch, we came to an agreement. I invited him to a local pub for lunch. Once we were settled with our beer, crisps and cheese sandwiches, we spoke about other matters.

He spoke about his interest in collecting antique items and that he was a member of the collectors' club. I mentioned my wife's friend's husband was an antique dealer. When I asked him if, by any chance, he knew Harold Nolan, he burst out laughing.

"Know him? In the club, we call him 'Harold hard-head."

This gave me the opening to enquire how Harold came to join a club that was basically for amateurs. It seemed that

27

Harold had put himself forward as an expert advisor whom the members might find useful. He also made a substantial financial contribution, which the club treasurer was delighted to accept. Knowing Harold, I'm sure it was put down as expenses for tax purposes.

Also, the club members were potential customers. I asked George if Harold was the only professional member. There were two or three others who did not attend the monthly meetings on a regular basis. We spoke about holidays and day trips. I was very interested in an upcoming trip to Shrewsbury on Friday. They wanted to visit an auction house where the main items for sale were antique clocks. This gave me an idea. I casually asked if Harold intended on going.

"Yes, he was the first one to put his name down on the list."

This was good news for me. I told George that I started my working life as an apprentice clock and watch repairer. One of my earliest jobs was to work on a clock that was four hundred years old and belonged to King Charles of France. Since then, right up to the present day, my interest was such that I converted the small bedroom into a clock workshop. One clock that I was working on at present was a mechanical four-hundred-day striking clock. There were only six ever made. I had worked on it when I was still an apprentice and persuaded the owner to sell it to me.

"Can you give me the address of the auction house?" I asked George.

"Tell you what. Why don't you come down with us?"

"I'd rather go on my own. I would like to give Harold a surprise when he sees me. I'm sure he will be well and truly miffed if I put up my four-hundred-day clock into the auction. Especially, as it is bound to fetch a very high return."

"So, what's it with you and Harold? We call him Harry the grump."

"It's like this. His wife and my wife have been close friends since university days. As you know, he tends to be a show-off. You've probably noticed that whatever you say, he will contradict. One way I get back at him, is I always wear my blazer with the RAF badge. This is a silent reminder that I did National Service whereas he did not, even though he is a few months older than me. My wife gets annoyed when the four of us go out together and no matter what fancy suit he wears, I wear my blazer. As well as that, Harold and I nearly always ended up having an argument no matter what the subject."

"I don't suppose that goes down well with your wives."

"You said it. Were it not for the fact that his wife Ann likes me a lot, I doubt if we would ever get together. Oh, and by the way, when I said Ann likes me, it's only in a platonic friendly way. Mind you, I'm sure it could go further if I were to take the initiative."

A little later, George and I went our separate ways and I phoned Jackie, confirming that I would be okay to go to America. In a nutshell, she said we should strike while the iron is hot and that I should be prepared to go at a moment's notice. I had to point out that early next week, I was scheduled to address a meeting of Ann's group. She reluctantly agreed that the America trip must not be later than the end of next week.

Of course, I do recognise that Jackie, as an agent, relies on the commission she receives from each book and the author she represents, and because she is comparatively new to the game, that's why she is keen. The first thing I had to do was check that my passport was up to date. Thankfully, it was.

Back home, Sandra was rushing about in the kitchen. "I've put some eggs out and bread in the toaster. Make yourself an omelette and a drink of coffee or whatever. Must dash. Got to get my gym clothes ready. Clive will be calling for me very soon."

"Oh, it's like that is it? I think our life is suddenly going to revolve around Clive. How did you go on this morning? Were you able to decide which nest of tables we are going to have?"

"Haven't got time to fill you in, except to say, we'll be having two sets, one for the TV room, the other for the front room."

One could say I was gob smacked. I moved slowly over to the counter where the eggs were and smashed them vigorously into a bowl. So much so, a few drops of yolk bounced up and hit me in the face. Two nests of tables! Thank goodness, Sandra did not want a new dining suite. I made a mental note to have words with Clive. The sooner the better. Just then, Sandra appeared. Never known her to get ready so fast.

"I would like to have a quick word with Clive before you two go dashing off."

"Sorry, my love. We'll only just make it in time even if he comes right now."

As if on cue, the beeping sound of a car interrupted our conversation. Once again, fate had struck against me. Before I could utter another word, Sandra went out to Clive's car. She had barely gotten in when it zoomed off. I must say that I do not like anything or anyone to interfere with my food, meals or appetite. This evening, however, it was a struggle.

I kept beating the eggs more than necessary. Also, couldn't stop muttering about how foolish I had been, which had resulted in a Sandra/Clive relationship. Or maybe, I was becoming paranoid. Should I or should I not speak to Joan about it? Would I appear as an absolute fool? Once again, in such a short time, I found myself on the horns of a dilemma. It took me some time before I settled down. I was just about to tackle my cheese with omelette, when my mobile summoned my attention. Jackie, speaking fast, blurted out that

30

we must leave Leeds next Wednesday in time to catch a night flight to New York. Angry by the fact that my meal was interrupted, I sharply pointed out that I had a long-standing arrangement to speak to Ann's group and in no way, would I let her down. After a fiery exchange of words, we compromised. I would have to cut my talk short. Jackie would pick me up from the location and together with another writer, who lived in Bradford, would belt down the M1.

By now, my omelette was too cold to eat. Still feeling miffed, I phoned Ann and explained the situation. I was relieved that she was so understanding. We agreed to alter the subject to a Question & Answer session about the current book or any other subject the audience so wished. So, another omelette later, with a large coffee and dare I say it, an even larger glass of whiskey, I settled down in front of the TV. To this day, I can't remember what I watched. I can remember going up the stairs, into pyjamas, switching on the radio and soon, head deep in the pillow, fell into a deep sleep. Utter bliss after the last few days of hectic happenings.

"Oy dozy head, time to get up. You mustn't be late for work. Come on shoo! Out of bed."

"Okay, Sandra! Give me at least a few seconds to wake up. I don't suppose you'd like to get me a bottle of fresh orange juice and a black coffee."

"You are absolutely right. I would not like to but I will."

It was too early in the morning for me to work out the implications of what she had just said. So, staggering into the bathroom, putting my head under the cold-water tap, I gradually reached normal, early-morning mode. In the kitchen, over breakfast, I told Sandra what had transpired with me, Jackie and Ann.

"You poor darling, all these women making life so hard for you. I don't know how you manage. As the old saying goes, 'it's tough at the top.'"

Sandra's voice, I can only describe as sweet sarcasm. A terrible thought struck me. I'll bet those nests of tables will be expensive. So, trying to sound nonchalant I said, "By the way, did Clive mention the cost for the nests of tables?"

"All he said was, you would be surprised when you read the invoice which he will send in a few days."

As I made my way to the front door, Sandra told me to wait a moment. She approached me, smiled, hugged me and gave me a sweet render kiss on the lips, as only she knew how.

"Have a really nice day."

Instead of enjoying the moment, all I could think of, was the size of the invoice. Damn it, another dilemma. If it will be a lot, then Sandra's nice approach was to soften the blow. On the other hand, if it would be cheap, how did Sandra persuade Clive to be so lenient? Had he, too, been a recipient of her delightful kiss and, perish the thought, even something more? Hells bells, why at my time of life, am I feeling so insecure? There was not much to do at the office so I spent the time trying to focus on my next novel. But, try as I might, nothing creative came to mind. I considered my pocket diary to when the trip to Shrewsbury would be. Couldn't find any date that mentioned it. I phoned George, who gave me the date. Thank goodness, it would be after I returned from the U.S.A. It also occurred to me that I had not arranged a date with Sandra for our night out at the Martins. I went on the internet to view their menus. If the quality of what was on offer was as good as their reputation, then it would be worthwhile. I forced myself not to look at the tariff. Although I was not entirely successful. I noticed a few that produced gulps in my throat. Still, if it meant making peace with Sandra, it would be worthwhile. By now, it was approaching lunchtime so I left a message with the secretarial staff that I was lunching early. Instead of nipping into the usual pub, I decided a pleasant stroll would be in order. The writer in me directed my feet to the nearest bookshop. I wondered if they stocked copies of Dilemma. I was not disappointed. A young lady was looking at a copy.

As she replaced it on the shelf, she noticed me and gave me a quizzical look. I realised what had happened. My picture on the back cover was still in her mind. I realised what was going on in her mind and said, "Yes, it is me. I am, for my sins, Don Donaldson."

"Nice to know you. I'm not sure if the story is my cup of tea. If you don't mind me saying so, the plot seems rather slow moving."

I couldn't think of a response. In the end, I came out with the old cliché, 'It takes all sorts.' I continued, "Do you do a lot of reading?"

"Yes. I'm reading English and English literature at university."

"So, I don't suppose you do any reading for pleasure?"

"You could say that. I spend some of my spare time either at the gym or swimming."

I looked at my watch. There was still time for some lunch. So, I asked her if she would like to join me at the usual pub for a beer and sandwich. She agreed, and in a short while, we were drinking, munching and exchanging views about writing. It transpired she liked poetry rather than prose. She suggested that perhaps it might help my writing if I included a few poems as part of the plot, say a dialogue between two characters. I thanked her for her advice and by the end of our time together, I felt good about myself. The only problem for me about poetry is that I know what I like but do not know what real poets understand by the deeper meanings involved. Back at the office, whilst dealing with some routine jobs, Jackie called in. I was surprised because although I'd told her where I worked, I did so on the understanding that she only contacts me via my mobile.

"Sorry to barge in, but we must bring our trip a day forward. A Hollywood top executive will be in New York next Tuesday."

I understood her point. However, how do I explain to Ann that I would have to cancel my talk? Again, another dilemma had reared its ugly head. No doubt, she would be annoyed, to say the least. Would she complain to Sandra about me? And as for Harold, he would be like the two-tailed dog gloating over the fact that I could not be relied upon. The only redeeming factor was the thought of eleven million dollars. I was about to phone Ann there and then, but decided against it. Perhaps, when I was back home, Sandra might come up with something. I was not disappointed.

"Have you been in touch lately with your old pal, Sid, the musical expert? Maybe he will be able to stand in for you?"

I lost no time in calling him. We had a chat about our current situation then explaining my situation, he was only too pleased to help me out. After that, I phoned Ann.

"I've some bad news and some good news for you, Ann. The bad news is, I can't make it for the talk. However, my friend, Sid, who is an expert on music, particularly on Opera, will stand in for me. Hope that's okay with you?"

I mentioned that Sandra had heard him speak a few times and was greatly impressed. At first, Ann didn't seem all that keen. But after I explained that Sid used CDs and the like, as part of his presentations, she was mollified. I suggested that after my America trip, I would make myself available. I said goodbye, but not before giving her Sid's contact details.

"Sandra, you have saved the day. Just for that tomorrow night, we'll be off to the Martins. What time should I book the table for?"

"I think eight would be just fine."

For the first time in a while, I was feeling fine. I promised Sandra that I would wear my best suit and not the RAF blazer outfit. Sandra was pleased because she had just bought a new evening dress that she wished to show off. I wonder why women must be so vain. I went on the internet and printed off some of the menus. Sandra looked at them but said that she'd choose when we were there. Come to think of it, perusing a menu could said to be, part of the eating-out ritual. After all, if the menu was large enough one, I could peep over the top and surreptitiously peep over the top at the other diners.

So, without further ado, I phoned through the booking. When I gave the young lady my name, she asked if I was the author of Dilemma. I gave her the good news but asked her not to broadcast the fact because I wanted the evening to be something special and intimate for me and my wife. She would do her best, providing, I would autograph her copy. She did explain that my presence would make for good publicity for the restaurant. I was reminded of one of the sayings of my late father, who was an expert observer of human nature. He used to say, 'nothing succeeds like successes'.

It was a busy morning at the office which made the time move fast. Rather than the usual pub lunch, I dashed off to the bookshop, had a look around, thumbed through some magazines. Noticed an advert about the Shrewsbury auction. This gave me an idea. I knew that this was one of the magazines that Harold had subscribed to. I took note of the editorial team's contact details. Back at the office, I had a coffee and phoned the magazine.

"Good afternoon. I'm Don Donaldson, the writer who started life as an apprentice for a clock and watch repairer. I would like to submit an article about that. Would you be interested?"

They agreed.

Chapter Two
A Night Out

During afternoon coffee break at the office, it struck me that the Martins may have a dress code for the evening meals. So, I phoned them. I was told that although there was no dress code as such, they preferred ladies in evening dresses and gentlemen in black tie or similar. The question was, should I hire something or just buy smart casual with a white frilly fronted shirt with perhaps a bootlace thin tie? Sandra would still be at her part-time job at the local school, so I couldn't contact her. I decided to go to the 'Men's Fashion boutique' that had just opened about a month ago. The modern background music did not help. I looked around, saw a young man and woman examining the stock rails. The young lady spotted me and came over.

"Is there anything special you are looking for, sir?"

I explained my predicament. She called over the young man. She asked him if he had any idea about the dress code at the Martins.

"We've had quite a few enquiries about that, sir, and I'm pleased to say we sold two outfits yesterday. I can show you what they went for."

My thought was, maybe he is just giving me a spiel to shift some slow-moving gear. On the other hand, perhaps he was telling the truth.

"This suit has a basic midnight-blue colour with the odd specs of light-blue. I understand this is all the rage in Paris."

"What about fancy shirt? I was thinking about one with a frilly front."

"We do have some, sir, but I don't think it would go with the suit. I see what you mean about not having a simple plain shirt. May I suggest a white shirt with a patterned collar and a hand painted tie? We have a big collection of ties."

I was not certain that my choice would meet Sandra's approval, so I enquired about their return policy.

"Providing none of the garments have been worn, we would accept them back. Depending on sales income, any refund might be in the form of vouchers or credit notes."

I thought this was a polite way of saying 'don't bring anything back'. After about half an hour, I made my choice and headed for home. When I arrived, Sandra was doing what women do when preparing to go out. I decided to hold back showing her my purchases because Sandra in preparation mode was for her a high-tension situation. I called out, "I'm going to have my shower now, okay?"

"Yes, okay don't bother me now."

I smiled, grabbed a towel and shaver and began undressing. Then I laid out my new clothes, chose an aftershave and a body spray. I calculated that I could spend at least half an hour in the shower and another twenty to get dressed. It was such a pleasure having a long hot shower, listening to some golden oldies being dished out on the radio. After finishing showering, I sprayed a liberal amount of body spray all over. Then, a slight mini-panic. I hadn't decided which shoes to wear and all of them were due for a polish. I was lucky that the first pair of black shoes were just right for dancing on the smallish space at the restaurant. So with a quick rub with my current vest, they shone up well.

Movement from upstairs. This could only mean Sandra was either finishing stage two or starting stage three. This involved trying on various garments and an 'I'm not sure why

I ever bought this. I hardly ever wear it. I should have taken it back to the shop, mode.' By now, I was fully dressed and couldn't help looking into the mirror and exclaiming 'Donald, you magnificent beast! How do you manage to look so handsome, you devilish wonder?' It was now time to switch on the kettle. I called out to Sandra, "Do you want a tea or coffee?"

"Give me five minutes. I'll have it in the back room."

"Okay, but when you say it, do you mean tea or coffee?"

"I'll have a fruit tea."

"Oh, by the way, I'm going to book a taxi. I don't want you driving because the chances are we'll both be having a lot to drink."

As I was preparing the drinks, I could hear Sandra coming down the stairs. As I went in the back room, there was Sandra, looking beautiful. I stood still, opened-mouthed. "It might help if you put the cups down instead of doing an impression of a statue."

I just stood there and blurted out, "Wow, Sandra! You look terrific! What a fab dress! Must have cost a fortune. Tell you what, I'll pay for it."

What else could I have done? The dress was figure hugging, put not too much. The material was a metallic purple with slight frilly top straps, light turquoise that revealed just enough cleavage to be interesting and, dare I say it, highly tempting. With her shoulder length, dark wavy hair and her exceptionally large, dark eyes, my youthful desires were beginning to rekindle.

"You should have warned me you were going to dress to kill. I'm running out of breath."

Sandra smiled and blew me a kiss. "There is one thing I must say, Don."

"What's that?"

"For heaven's sake, put the drinks down before you spill them."

I complied and sat down.

"I see you are wearing something I haven't seen before. Have you been buying clothes without me being there to advise?" I stood up.

"That's right. But what else could I do? I checked with the Martins and they do have a dress code for the evening. And I wasn't sure that what I have would be suitable."

"I suppose that's an acceptable excuse. Turn around, slowly. Well, on the whole, you did fairly well on your own but please don't make a habit of it."

"What do you think of the tie?"

"It's not what I would have chosen. Did they have any others?"

"Yes, but I thought the colours of this tie were the best suited for the rest of the ensemble."

"Rest of the ensemble, my, my! We are going up the world now that we are an accomplished author."

Not knowing just how to respond to Sandra's use of the royal wee, I said maybe I'll phone for the taxi. We didn't have long to wait. So, for the twenty minutes' drive, we made ourselves comfortable on the rear seats, holding hands, something we had not done for many years. I guess that I'd been forgiven completely for the last time we were out to dinner.

The taxi driver was one of those who liked to chat. He suggested that we were going out on a special occasion. It was this sort of enquiry that annoys me. In my opinion, it is the height of impudence. I thought the best way to put him down was to answer that a dinner was being held in my honour because of me being the bestselling author of the book entitled 'Dilemma'. I then added, "I suppose you've bought a copy". He said no and kept silent for the rest of the journey.

When we reached our destination, a uniformed doorman opened the taxi door and helped Sandra out. I did not tip the taxi driver. Never having been to the Martins, I was impressed by, what in other places, would have been the foyer. Here, however, was a large reception lounge. Must have been about thirty tables with four chairs to a table. A beautifully designed artistic notice asked patrons to approach the reception desk where three very attractive uniformed ladies were seated. Upon telling them who we were, one of them escorted us to the dining area. I couldn't help but notice the frowns of the other patrons who were seated at the reception tables. Who knows how long they must have been waiting! Sandra remarked that there are advantages being married to a bestselling writer.

What impressed me was the layout of the dining area. Circular tables with placed mats that showed pictures of different species of Martins. The condiment containers were made of different geometrical shapes and pastel colours. The chairs, although basic dining chairs, were upholstered in such a way that they looked like mini armchairs. The most appealing aspect in my opinion was the fact that one could view what was happening outside the building. The smallish dance floor was still large enough to allow six or seven couples to dance at the same time.

We were given a choice of three tables at which to sit. Sandra asked about the location of the ladies restroom. She chose the table farthest way. This allowed her to parade the longest distance whereby she could show off her fabulous figure. She did this almost straight away as we were seated and handed the menus. Nearly all the male diners strained their necks to get a good look at her. One poor chap was struck in the face by the woman he was with. She grabbed her napkin and, with a mighty swish, hit her target. When Sandra made her way back to our table, the gentlemen diners just allowed their eyes to follow her, whist their female companions either scowled or looked daggers. Sandra just smiled at me and asked if I had decided what to order. At that moment, a waiter came over and placed an ice bucket of champagne on the tables.

"I didn't order champagne," I protested on the assumption that he had brought it to the wrong table. "Compliments of the management, Mr Donaldson."

He poured out the two glasses and we toasted each other. It was difficult for me. No fish and chips on the menu. My eye was drawn to an item 'Old-fashioned meat pie'. Sandra said she had no idea what it consisted of, so she called over the waiter and asked him. He explained that it was one of the chef's own specialty. It consisted of various ends of meats plus shallots, onions and garlic and a touch of mixed herbs. I thought I would give it a try. Sandra was concerned that whatever she ordered would not, by chance, spill on her new dress. I suppose we all have our individual priorities. As the cream of tomato soup we both ordered came to the table, a young man and woman ascended the three steps to the keyboard and microphone.

"Ladies and gentlemen, before we begin the evening's entertainment, it gives me great pleasure to invite a surprise celebrity guest, the well-known author, Don Donaldson, to join me on-stage."

I rose and took Sandra by the hand.

"Come on, beautiful, you are coming with me."

At first she was reluctant, but gradually walked with me to the stage. But not before I pointed out that this was another opportunity to parade her lovely figure.

"I don't know what you mean. Do you really think I'm some sort of a show-off?"

"My darling, all women are basically show-offs and you have much more to show off than most women."

41

By this time, we had reached the stage accompanied by a little mild applause.

"So, Don. How are things going with you since you made the bestseller list?"

"It is hectic now, but thanks to the steadying hand of my very lovely wife, Sandra, I'm just about on even keel."

"So, Sandra, what's it like, keeping your celebrity husband on the straight and narrow?"

"The way I can describe is, I know what he likes to do. He knows that if he doesn't toe the line, he'll not get what he likes. Also, he knows that if I don't get what I want, there will be trouble ahead."

This brought various sounds from the diners. Some just laughed, others applauded, a few banged their hands on their tables.

"So, tell us, Don, what next?"

"Next week I'm off to the States for a non-stop three or four days' book-signing tour. I'm told Dilemma is going great guns over there."

"Well, thank you for being with us. Ladies and gentlemen, a big hand for Don and Sandra."

We returned to our table, as slowly as possible, thereby giving Sandra more show-off time. Thank goodness, the soup was still warm enough to eat. As we were beginning to eat, a young woman came to our table.

"Sorry to disturb you. I spoke to you this afternoon over the phone. I'm the editor of Modernatique Times. I would like to speak to you when you have finished your meal. Is that okay?"

"Okay, sure."

"What's that all about?" Sandra asked.

"I was browsing this lunchtime in the bookshop near the office and I came across the magazine she mentioned. I called her when I got back to work and suggested I could write an article about antique clocks for the next issue."

"Is there any particular reason why that magazine and not another?"

"Two reasons. First, there was an article in the current issue about the auction of antique clocks next Monday in Shrewsbury. I did mention to you that I would be going there."

"I'm sure you did not."

Sandra sounded surprised but not angry.

"Well, with all the hectic activity at work and the trip to America, it must have slipped my mind. Sorry about that. Mind you, if you can get time off, why don't you come with me?"

"We are too busy at school all next week, although if I'd have known sooner, I might have been able to make arrangements."

"I didn't know myself, till yesterday. The new account that I secured yesterday is run by George Smith who is a member of an Antiques club and guess who else is a member?"

"Go on, surprise me."

"None other than our old friend, Harold."

Sandra replaced her spoon on the table and gave me a sharp look.

"By any chance, are you trying to do something to upset him?"

"I wouldn't exactly say that."

"And just what is that supposed to mean? I haven't had time to get in touch with Ann, don't want you to make matters worse."

"This is the thing. I know that Harold and the group will be going to Shrewsbury for the auction. And I want to sell that four hundred day striking clock that I was overhauling at home. It is bound to fetch a high price and I must admit, the

43

thought crossed my mind that would probably upset Harold. I can't be held responsible if my success with an antique might annoy Harold."

A thought occurred. For some reason, I took out my diary and checked the date of the auction.

"I've made a mistake, Sandra. The auction does not take place till the Monday after I return from America."

I cleared that up with Sandra. The rest of the evening went well. The close dancing with Sandra made me feel on top of the world. Her perfumes emanating from her hair and cheeks. I wanted there and then to dash back home and enjoy the sheer feminine delights that she exuded when we were courting. I never in my wildest moments, think we could reignite that fantastic pleasure. As we were dancing, I kept having twinges of guilt about the last time we were with Harold and Ann.

As we returned to our table for the coffee cheese and crackers, I said to her, "You know what, Sandra, I don't deserve you. I'll never know why you have put up with me. I spend so much time writing or working on my clocks, I hardly ever see you and we don't do many things together. I wish there was some way I could make it up to you." She looked across at me, smiled, leaned over and kissed me.

"If you really want to make it up to me, all you have to do is let me take control of the eleven million dollars—or its equivalent in Sterling."

At that moment, the editor of Modernatique Times came over.

"Is it all right if I speak to you now?"

I looked at Sandra. She nodded her approval.

"Can you give me details of how you came to be interested in Antique clocks?"

I told her about my apprenticeship. She then asked me if I could let her have my article no later than next Monday. I agreed, then asked her if she could arrange for my photo together with Sandra's to be on the front cover of the Magazine. There and then, she took six photos of us with her hand-held minicomputer. She couldn't promise that we would appear on the front cover, but one or maybe two photos would be included somewhere.

After she returned to her table, Sandra asked me why I was so particular for our picture to be featured on the front cover. When I told her the answer, she was not really pleased but could not suppress a smile. The reason was that Harold's group subscribed to the magazine. So, what better way to annoy him by seeing my picture on the front cover.

As the waiter came over with bill, he asked us how we would be getting home. When I said by taxi, he said the Management would provide a complimentary taxi. It seems they have a special contract with one of the biggest taxi firms. Thank Heavens, we had a quiet taxi driver for the return journey. We snuggled up close. Back home, Sandra said, "I've been having difficulty with the zip of my dress, probably because it's new. Do you think you might be able to undo it without too much trouble?"

"I'll certainly do my very best to oblige."

"Oh and there is something else. You'd better think of an excuse as to why you will be late in the morning."

I can only describe what followed as sheer bliss. Or to put it another way, every memory and love fantasy that I had experienced came together. The combination of Sandra's perfume, the music and the comedy film we watched combined to make the perfect atmosphere that I think will never be repeated. As for breakfast, during which the night's activities still clung in my mind, made the coffee and orange juice taste better than ever. How could I possibly leave Sandra for a week or so? It took all my mental reserves not say 'To hell with writing. I've just got to be with Sandra. She is my reason for living.' My thoughts were interrupted as Sandra entered the kitchen.

"Well, my tiger. Did you enjoy your breakfast?"

Although she had washed and dressed, removed all the makeup from her big, ever-fascinating eyes, they still had their magic power over me. For a few seconds, I just leaned back in my chair.

"Enjoy! I'm on the verge of phoning my agent and telling her that I have given up writing and, if no more copies sell, well too bad. I have everything I want here in front of me."

Sandra, as sharp as ever, in a seductive whisper, leaning over me said, "I can think of eleven million reasons why you should not cancel your trip." She then added, "Besides, I need time for my interests too. That reminds me I must change into leotards. Clive is booking us both into a new super gym. So, off you go to the office. Don't forget the editor of that magazine will be coming to see you."

All I could imagine was, if an old man like me can be aroused to distraction, goodness knows what effect Sandra's looks would have on young, virile Clive. So, as I was putting on my raincoat and hat, I left home muttering all the way to the bus stop. Dilemma after dilemma. How come after all these years, I'm so insecure? It's not as though if I saw an attractive woman I would shut my eyes and pretend not to see her. I had to be brutally honest with myself. If the opportunity came my way, I know I would make a pass. So, what right did I have to think badly about Sandra? Maybe I should consult a therapist of some kind. Then again, what would he or she say to me that I have not already told myself?

As I stepped onto the bus, I felt a little better, but still couldn't help thinking about how terrific Sandra looks these days. I convinced myself that there was more chance of her making out with another man, than there was for me attracting another woman. Damn it! Is it the truth that deep down I'm jealous of Sandra? I'll bet that's the conclusion an expensive session with a therapist would tell me. I smiled and laughed ironically. I'd just saved myself a fortune by not consulting a therapist. I felt even better when I thought on what I could spend the savings I had just made. Perhaps a few shirts and ties for the American trip.

It was fortunate that when I reached the office, the boss was out. This gave me time to settle down and head for the coffee machine. By the time I was back at my desk, the editor of Modernatique Times had arrived.

"Thanks for calling. By the way, I don't know your name."

"I'm Valarie, but the rest of the world calls me Val."

"Okay, Val it is. So, what do you want to know about me?"

"Start with a short bio of how you came to be a writer and your connection with antique clocks."

"Well, in primary school, I was not very bright. In fact, the teacher divided the class into groups. A, B, C, D, and Mugs Alley. This was a real downer for me. I felt a deep sadness and a total lack of self-confidence. However, I always amazed the teacher when I achieved top marks for History and Geography. He would call me over to his desk and say, "Why can't your English and Math be like your History and Geography? You simply don't try." I couldn't think of an answer so, with a sheepish look on my face, he would send me back to my desk. Years later, in the lower secondary class, we were given a composition to write. After we handed in what we had written, the teacher said, "There is one piece that I have marked very good. Please come out, the boy who wrote it." Nobody moved. I just stared into space. After a few seconds and still no one moved. The teacher became angry and said in a firm voice, "Everybody look into your exercise book now." So I complied; and there it was, in big red letters 'V. Good'. With shaking hands, open-mouthed, I stepped forward. He asked me to read my composition. He then went on to explain to the class why it was so good. This, for me, was a spurt and a shove. From then on, it became a matter of pride that I would, from then on, make a point of always being top in English. I'm pleased to say that's how it was 'till I left school."

"So, how did and when did your interest in antique clocks begin?"

"In those days, at age fifteen, we had to leave school and get a job. I became an apprentice of a Watch and Clock repairer. One of the main customers was a well-known antique dealer, who specialised in old and unusual clocks. You know, I suppose that there is an auction in Shrewsbury scheduled in a few weeks' time. I'll be submitting for sale one four hundred day striking clock that I over-hauled some time ago.

It was interesting how I came to own it. A man came into the shop where I was employed. He asked how much it would cost to repair. There were some parts needed and it needed much work to be done on it. When told the estimate, he said he couldn't afford it and asked how much my boss would be prepared to take it off his hands. They agreed on a price, I forgot how much. A short while later, the boss went bankrupt. Before closing down the business, he asked if I wanted anything for myself. I asked for the clock and several tools. I'm only sorry there was not enough room in my parents' home that would accommodate all the stuff I would have liked to have taken."

"One more question. Besides clocks, are there any other types of antiques that interest you?"

"As a writer, any old book in good condition. And there was a time when I took an interest in woodwork."

"Thank you, Donald. I'll see what I can do about getting you on the front cover but I can't promise. We'll send you a cheque for your article in about a week or so."

With that, we bid each other goodbye. And I spent the rest of the afternoon on the phone trying to promote business. I was, I'm pleased to say, successful. I was feeling good. I thought perhaps I'd call-in for a quick drink before going home. I got up from my chair, went over to the coat hanger, and just as I was halfway putting on my coat, guess what? That damn mobile sprang into action. It was my agent. "Sorry to bother you now. I guess you must be on your way home. Thing is, I need to speak to you a.s.a.p. Are you available first thing tomorrow? Say, about eight prompt?"

"Sure, no problem."

"Okay, see you then. Bye for now."

That settled it. I went for a drink and wasted time trying to fathom out what could possibly be so urgent that would demand an early morning meeting? There was still a week to go, so why all the fuss? I would have swallowed the remaining half of my drink then dashed off for the bus home. A tap on the shoulder made me halt in my tracks. I turned around. Someone who I'd not seen since leaving school was standing next to me, pint glass in hand, asking me what the rush was and invited me to have another with him. It was my old pal Kevin. He'd certainly broadened out since the school leaving party. Come to think of it, I too had put on a bit of weight since then.

"Kevin, my old mate, I'd heard that you and your family have up sticks and gone to Australia. What brings you back to dear old Blighty?"

"We are just here for a funeral. Wife's eldest sister passed away. Anyway, we thought we'd stop for a few more weeks and look up old friends and places. I see you've done well with your bestseller."

"Can't complain. I'm off to America next week. My agent's firm is paying for it. They think that Hollywood is almost certain to buy the film rights off me. We are looking at an eleven-million-dollar contract. I'm not sure how much that is in Sterling. So, tell me what have you been up to since we last met?"

"Not quite as good as you. After leaving school, I got a job in a garage. Studied for City and Guilds. Managed to pass but, don't mind telling you, it was a struggle. You know what I was like at school, not too bright in the classroom, but something of a jimmy whizz at sport."

"Yes, you are right. Like me, you made first thirteen in the school Rugby League team and the first eleven at Cricket. Do you get to see much Cricket in Australia?"

"Not half! I'm the secretary of a local club that coaches youngsters amongst other things."

"As I remember, you were the only all-rounder in our school team. I was okay as a fast opening bowler but lousy at batting. Mind you, I don't suppose you recall that game where I actually made double figures."

"Oh yes, that was in the semi-final of the Hare hills shield. We went on to win the shield. I hit the winning run."

"They were great days. You know the old saying 'School days are the happiest days of your life'".

"Don't know about that. I'd say my best days are still happening. Got smashing wife and three kids that keep me busy. Never a dull moment. What about you do you have family?"

"Yes, a son and daughter. Mind you, we never see them. My son lives in London. He has two lads. And my daughter with her two, lives in Paris. Although as I say, we don't see them but thanks to the Internet, we are in touch at least once a month. Can't imagine how we managed before e-mail, Facebook and such like. So, what are you doing besides coaching the future Aussie Test team?"

"I'm partners with a guy. We run a garage and scrap yard. With a bit of luck, we could be expanding. By that I mean, we may open a place in Melbourne. We live in Sydney."

I looked at my watch.

"Well, Kevin, as much as I would like to stay and chat, I really must be going. Give me your e-mail add and we'll keep in touch. By the way, have had a look at the old places we grew up in?"

"I have. Boy, how it's changed, and not for the good."

I had to agree with him. We exchanged e-mail ads. When I reached home, Sandra was not there. So I started peeling potatoes for the evening meal. I was looking forward to chops and roast veg. Had just finished and was about to tackle the onions when Sandra returned.

"Boy, I am I glad to see you."

"Now, now, tiger, be patient. Control your passion. Just relax."

"Sorry Sandra, it's not my passion that's been aroused. It's a thought that you can peel the onions. You know, that try as I might, I cannot avoid sting tears no matter what method I use to peel them."

"And there was I, thinking that you've been dying all day thinking about me and wanting to vent your lust on me."

"Actually, you are right. But onion peeling? Yuk!"

"Very well," she said in a comical tone of voice, "I'll just have to be disappointed."

Soon the chops were crackling in the frying pan and just as we were about to enjoy dinner, the phone rang.

"Did you put the answer phone on?" I enquired. Sandra shook her head.

"Did you?"

I thought it best that I should take the blame.

"Silly me. Went clean out of my head. Will you answer it or shall I?"

Sandra said she would, because her chair was nearest to the phone.

"It's your agent. She wants to come around. Has something urgent to speak about."

"Damn and blast! We already arranged that she would see me at the office tomorrow at eight. What the hell could have happened in the meantime? Tell her I'm out or in the loo."

Sandra smiled a broad grin.

"He's not here right now but I'm expecting him back in an hour or so. Is that okay? Right, I take it you know where we live. I see. Where will you be coming from? In that case, make for the ring road, when you reach the moor town roundabout, turn left and we are on the third turning on the left at the bottom of the hill. Okay bye for now."

"Sandra, you are a star. To celebrate, let's enjoy our meal."

The meal started. I opened two cans of lager.

"Can't think why she couldn't wait till tomorrow it seems so..."

Sandra interrupted, "Stop talking, enjoy your chops. She'll be here in a bit; you'll know soon enough."

We had barely time to clear the table when the front door bell rang. I opened the door and there was Jackie. She was not alone. I invited them in.

"Don, this is Jo Abbots, think you may have heard of her. She writes women's romances."

I had to confess that I hadn't but suggested that Sandra might have. I showed them into the lounge where Sandra was pouring out coffee for herself and a lemon tea for me. After introducing them, Sandra asked if they would like a drink. They both asked for tea. Sandra went into the kitchen.

"Right Jackie. What gives?"

Her reply made me gulp.

"There has been a change in plan. Later tonight, we need to be in Amsterdam to take the flight to Toronto. The thing is, for technical reasons, plus the fact that tomorrow a whole production Hollywood team will be in New York. So, have a look at these notes. Jo already has her copy."

My mind was all of a whirl. How could my absence be explained to my boss? Why was Jo coming with us? Why does a magazine writer need to go on a book signing tour? Jackie must have read my mind.

"I've cleared your departure with your firm. I spoke to your boss before coming here. Jo is coming because the wife of the top director thinks that some of her stories would make good films."

I must admit, if Jackie's agency could afford to pay for Jo, then why not Sandra also? At that moment, I was feeling miffed. A good job Sandra returned from the kitchen. I turned to Jackie.

"So, what time is the flight to Amsterdam?"

"We've plenty of time. It leaves Yeadon at half past eleven."

By now, I was feeling somewhat calmer. Sandra said she would pack a change of clothes for me. It was already eight o 'clock. I was hoping for a shower and an early night. That, however, was not to be. In the end, Jackie, Jo and I drove off to Jackie's flat that was near the airport. I managed to have a shower there. Afterwards, we went through the itinerary notes. We were scheduled to reach Toronto at eight, local. At the airport we would be met by a radio and TV teams for the good day early morning programs. A stall with some copies of 'Dilemma' would be set up for a book signing session. Then, a quick dash to the coach for New York. Once in New York, a quick breakfast at the nearest diner where Jackie would call up the Radio and TV teams for interviews. From then on, we'd play it by ear. For the book signing, a rubber stamp of my autograph would be made. I pointed out to Jackie that I liked to inscribe something that would make the reader feel that he or she was special. Jackie said that would not be possible because of the time factor. I was, however, insistent that somehow we must make time. I hit on an idea.

"I've an idea. I'll write out some phrases that could be made into rubber stamps just like my autograph."

She was reluctant but agreed.

So, I wrote: 'Enjoy the book', 'Hope you like the story', 'my next Novel will be just as good' and finally 'pleased you like reading.'

I could tell Jackie was not at all happy with my input, but I stood firm. I told her this is part of who I am and some way must be found to accommodate my wishes. In the end, she made a few phone calls. I went on her computer, e-mailed the four phrases and felt rather good about it. After all, in this day and age of electronic communication, how long would it take to implement the task? A little later, Jackie went through the rest of the schedule.

"If you turn to page three, you'll see we have a brainstorming all day session for writers. You will be conducting it and perhaps, somehow, you could involve Jo. Off the top of your head, can you think of how you will conduct it?"

"I take that, this is over and above the book signing project which means I should be entitled to a fee?"

Jackie's face turned into a frown.

"I suppose something could be arranged."

It was my turn to frown. This project was turning out to be something of an ordeal. I made a point of bearing in mind that there were eleven million good reasons to stick to it. So, I decided to use 'Dilemma' as a text for constructive analysis. By that, I mean I would ask a member of the audience to read out one of the chapters and put questions to the audience, asking how they would adapt the story as a radio play or a TV production. Perhaps, even stage plays. Although, on second thoughts, the scenes where the two main characters were in the next world would be hard to show on a live stage. In the end, I thought it would be good as a challenge to their ingenuity. As far as Jo was concerned, I thought she could conduct a session on the techniques of short story writing. We agreed that this event would be on the last day of my visit. As I was looking through the rest of the itinerary, I could not figure out how it would be possible for all the interviews to be fitted in. Still, that was Jackie's problem, not mine.

At the brainstorming, the Hollywood team were present. We had a working lunch. The main points under discussion were, which parts could be left out to fit in with a two-hour film and who should play the main characters. Half way through lunch, the screenplay writers left. There was just me, Jackie and the two executives. We spoke about payment. Jackie opened up by saying that in her discussions, a proposal of around eleven million dollars was suggested. The financial executive said that since then, the situation had changed and that they could only offer eight million. I was prepared there and then to accept. Jackie, however, was not pleased and said so in no uncertain terms. I realised that the lower the offer would mean less commission for her and her agency. So, he came up with a counter offer. Eight million, plus a percentage of the takings each time the film was shown. Once again, I was delighted with the offer. Not so Jackie. As far as she was concerned, it would depend on the percentage. There was a lot of argument with Jackie insisting that the percentage was far too low and unacceptable. Maybe I was wrong but I felt I had to say something. I put it to them: I'd be prepared to accept the takings offer, provided the cash sum could be raised to nine million dollars. Jackie looked daggers at me. The executive took out his calculator, punched in a few numbers and looked at Jackie. The final offer would be a slight increase in the percentage but the cash would be eight and a half million. Jackie looked at me and asked in a soft tone how I felt about that. The daggers had disappeared from her eyes. A short while later and the contract was signed. The only thought that came to mind was, if Sandra and I did not go over the top, we could spend the rest of our lives in luxury and comfort. At that moment, I was at the apex of my happiness. No more financial worries, time could be spent on my other interests and hobbies. Must not forget, son and daughter as well as grandchildren.

Before all this took place, when we were settled in our seats, taking off from Schiphol, I got to know Jo really well. When the plane levelled out and we were taking sips of coffee and whiskey, the quality of both left much to be desired, still at these prices one shouldn't complain. Jo and I were seated next to each other. Perhaps, it was the whiskey that affected her or the night flight. Whichever it was, I couldn't help but notice the tears welling up in her eyes.

"Jo, are you feeling okay?"

She turned to face me full on and the outburst started. I put my arm around her and drew her close, very close. I took advantage of the situation and her shapely feminine charms. I hasten to add purely as an act of sympathy.

"Nice and easy, Jo, just tell me nice and slow, just what the problem is?"

"It says in the notes that I, like you, must conduct part of the brainstorming session. It takes time to prepare something like that."

I kissed her on the cheek and noticed how nice she smelled.

"You are right about that. I think I have a solution if you are agreeable."

She squeezed my hand and sighed, "Okay, tell me what's on your mind."

"When I go on the stage or whatever it is, you will accompany me. I'll explain to the writers that you are an accomplished short story writer who will be pleased to answer any questions about the art of short story writing. Then, I'll speak about your background and which magazines you have written for. After that, I'll ask which of your stories gave you the most pleasure and why. Then, Jo, you'll be on your own for as long or as short as it takes. How does that grab you?"

Her reaction was one I did not expect. She sat back, looked at me, smiled and kissed me firmly on the lips. "Donald, you are absolutely marvellous."

As if by magic, my mobile announced an e-mail coming in. Before looking at it, I thought maybe I should have switched it off. It's hard to keep up with all the rules and regulations re personal electronic gadgets and airlines. I should have known. It was from Sandra. It simply said, 'Save all your strength for me, tiger.'

I'll swear Sandra has a super sixth sense that can detect any beautiful woman that comes within kissing distance, no matter how far we are apart.

The rest of the journey, I and my beautiful blonde companion snuggled up together under the blankets provided by the airline. We were brought back to reality by the gentle bounce of the aircraft as it landed and taxied to the arrival lounge. It took sometime before we were brought to the reception for our first appearance of the tour. We were lead into the V.I.P. lounge where the TV cameras were set up. I said we needed to freshen up so we were shown the way to the washrooms. When we returned, Jackie was already speaking to the journalists. She called me over.

"And now, here we have at the microphone, Don Donaldson himself."

"So, Don, you have a busy tight schedule ahead. How do you think you'll cope?'

"The only real problem I have, is that my time here in Canada has to be so short. I often look at various places in Canada via the internet and have always planned to come here. I know there is a lot to see."

I thought it would be diplomatic and expedient to praise the place where I was.

"I see you still have about five minutes or so before travelling to the States, so if you follow me where you can autograph copies of 'Dilemma'."

There were more people there than I expected. Hard to say what the average age was. I noticed somewhere in the middle of the group were two chair-bound people who were waving their books. I made my way to them. Both were middle-aged. A man and a woman. As I was signing, I asked them if there was any chance of a recovery for them. Both shook their heads.

"Any particular type of stories you like?"

The lady said she liked romances the best. I called Jo over to her and made sure the photographers saw them together. I think I managed to sign about twenty odd copies before Jackie shoved us off to the coach. Before entering, I turned to the crowd and shouted that I was working on another novel and hoped they would buy a copy. Sitting next to Jo, I rather sheepishly asked how she was coping with the trip. She leaned close and whispered directly in my ear, "Bearing up, thanks to you."

I replied, "I'm always ready to assist in any way."

I winked with a knowing smile. We were taken to task by Jackie who was seated directly behind us.

"Will you two love birds please concentrate on the job in hand? We have a very busy morning and you must focus on the programme."

Jo and I grinned softly.

"That's what we are doing, Captain." I said mischievously. A few passengers came up to us for autographs. At first, they only wanted mine. I told them that a few of Jo's stories were going to be made into blockbuster film in the not-too-distant future. We reached New York just in time for the morning hustle and bustle. A good-job Jackie was on the ball because no sooner had we alighted the coach, when a Taxi drew up and we were on the way to the hotel. I was glad to unpack and shower. The girls had a double room adjoining mine. We were no sooner washed and in a change of clothes when Jackie took us on a walkabout. What I didn't realise, was that this was an election year in the U.S. Not far from where we were walking, two teams of TV guys and gals were following the candidates. Jackie called out to one of the journalists, explaining who we were and that we were scheduled for an interview. There was some confusion for a while. Then, an enterprising young lady reporter from a radio station came over to us.

"We have two surprise visitors, our good morning N.Y. show All the way from Britain via Canada. I will speak to Don Donaldson, author of the bestselling novel 'Dilemmas'. So, Don what brings you to the States?"

"I'm here for a book signing session, or should I say sessions. Also I'll be conducting a brainstorming programme in a few days' time for up and coming would-be writers."

"Yes, your agent has just informed that it costs one hundred dollars, a ticket including lunch. So, if you writers out there want to take advantage of this, what is perhaps a once in a lifetime opportunity to meet and speak to a top class bestselling author, contact this radio station. I'm told there are still some tickets left, so hurry while there is still time."

I decided to interrupt.

"Also, you will have the chance to speak to Jo Abbot, the well-known short story writer, who specialises in romantic stories."

Jackie signalled that it was time for us to move on. She guided us to a Deli Diner for breakfast. We ordered coffee, orange juice, bagels with Lox and two fried eggs. The girls too were ravenous. I don't know what it is about me, but as soon as I start to eat, invariably I'm always interrupted. Today was no exception. In came one of the candidates, followed by an entourage of TV cameras and microphones. "So, my friends, will you be voting for me and my party? "Most definitely not. I and my two lady friends are visitors from Britain, here to promote my bestselling novel 'Dilemmas'."

"Well, I hope all goes well for you. But tell me, do you believe in a free market economy?"

"If you mean like what you have here in the States, it would not be ethical as a foreign visitor to express an opinion because I and my friends are guests here."

"I think you would make a good politician."' Smiling and proceeded to speak to the other diners.

Jackie said I handled that very well. From then on, all that day, it was one big dash from one book store to the next. In two places, scuffles broke out when it came time to leave. Although the signing was meant just for my book, I did my best when ladies came forward. I asked if they read romantic short stories or novels. Most of them said yes, so I pointed to Jo saying, "This is Jo Abbot, you must have read some of her stories." It so happened they did, but only those who had brought their autograph books were lucky enough to get a signature. Some enterprising women rushed over to the stationery counter and bought a note pad. Perhaps, this is what caused the slowdown in our itinerary which upset Jackie. The working day lasted till just past ten p.m. Back in the hotel, freshening up, I invited Jo to join me in the bar for a cocktail and a few snacks.

"Thanks, Don, but I think you should ask Jackie as well." I protested and said she would be too busy working on tomorrow's events.

"Oh, Don, why is it men are so slow to catch on? You must have noticed how she always has a dig at us when we spend time together."

"No, not really. I'm sure she was joking."

"So, you don't think she fancies you?"

"Surely not. My son and daughter are older than her and my grandchildren are not far off her age."

"Take my advice. Go and ask her now. I'm not sure how she'll react. But it'll show you are not ignoring her."

Against my better judgement, I did what Jo advised. I was not prepared for the onslaught that ensued. I knocked on the door. Jackie called out, "Who is it?"

"Only me, Jackie."

She invited me in. I asked her if she would like to join me and Jo in the Cocktail Bar for a relaxing time out.

"I'm not in the habit of playing gooseberry"

. Her tone was sharp. I was taken aback because in all the time I'd known her, she'd never shown any type of angry emotion.

"What do you mean gooseberry? I don't understand what you are implying." I was truly shocked.

"Come off it, Don. Admit it, you are cheating on your wife with that man-eating slut."

I could feel my hackles rising but managed almost to keep anger out of my next comment.

"Jackie, you know very well that I am a man of ethical principles. There is no way I would ever consider cheating on Sandra."

61

"What would you call putting your arms around Jo, exchanging kisses, bringing her in to your book signing session, and giving her free publicity on the radio interview that was intended for you and you only? Oh and by the way, do your ethical principles permit you to cheat with a married woman?"

"Excuse me. Are saying that Jo is married? She does not wear a ring."

"Not only is she married, she's been divorced twice. Where do you think she gets her plot lines for her stories? They are based on the affairs she's had. Oh, whist you are here, you might as well know now. I don't want to be your agent anymore. As soon as we are back home, that's it."

That threw me completely. So, probably out of shock, I blurted out, "That's fine by me. As soon as the Hollywood deal is completed and the money is in my bank, that's it. No more writing professionally for me. I'll have more time to be with Sandra and my other hobbies."

"By other hobbies, do you mean chasing other sluts?"

"You know what Jackie. I am really disappointed in you. I never thought you could be a vicious, vindictive person." With that, I turned away and went down to the cocktail bar. Jo was seated at a corner table sipping what looked like a whiskey sour. She looked up, a broad beaming smile on her face.

"Will Jackie be joining us later?"

Once again, another dilemma. Do I keep quiet about my confrontation with Jackie? Or do I, as diplomatically as possible, tell Jo what took place? Taking a sip of her whiskey sour, she glanced up and saw me approaching. Her expression, a slight knowing smile which widened when I neared the table.

"I take it your agent will not be joining us."

She sounded really pleased. I couldn't help wondering if they had words at some time about me. I'd never heard Jo refer to Jackie as my agent. I thought it best if I went on the attack.

"Have you and Jackie been arguing?"

"Well, let me put it this way. She took an instant dislike to me because of the way I came to be on this trip and looks for any pretext to show her dislike."

"I know you were invited because the wife of one of the Hollywood team is keen to meet you. Something about your stories she likes."

"Yes, that's right. But what you may not know, is Jackie's agency gets no commission on my activities. It was a case of 'if I don't come then the Hollywood deal would be cancelled and Jackie's commission would plummet'. You see, she is beholden to me and resents it."

This threw a new light on the situation. Jo must have known that by me asking Jackie to join us for cocktails, would annoy her a lot and I would have to bear the brunt of Jackie's displeasure.

So, now I'm being used as a weapon in a cat fight, and a target. Not the best of situations when tomorrow, the final day of the trip and the brainstorming event. It was going to take all my mental reserves to focus on the subject matter. I just prayed that the contract with Hollywood would not take long to be implemented and the money in my bank. It was just after nine o'clock. I could tell Jo must have had at least three cocktails. I called the waiter over and ordered a Bloody Mary. I had to think quickly. I must make sure the two cat fighters would concentrate on each other and leave me out of it. So I decided to ask Jo about her past.

"Is it true you have been divorced twice? And you are now married again?"

"So, the little minx has been spilling the beans. Does it make any difference to you? Does it still stop you from enjoying my company?"

Oh boy! Now one of the cats is turning on me.

"It would have, had I known. It's not my practice to go after married women. You do know that I am married with a son and daughter and four grandchildren."

"I was aware. I read your bio in a writing magazine. I wasn't surprised by your – shall we say your affection techniques. Some would say your lustful actions."

Once again, I found myself on the defensive.

"I don't know about you but I'll have another drink, then go to bed."

I needed to be fully relaxed and alert for tomorrow.'

"I know a first class technique for relaxing. So why don't I join you in on another cocktail in your room?"

With my head spinning and the thought of Sandra and Clive maybe enjoying each other's company, trying to justify what Jo had in mind. Should I, shouldn't I?

As if reading my mind, Jo said, "Even a married man with four grandchildren needs to relax sometimes."

A wicked smile and slightly pouting lips with bright eyes going into luring mode. I turned away from her and looked out at the moving traffic and flashing advert signs on the New York skyline. Then it struck me. Jo must have read the publicity about my Hollywood contract. Was planning a kiss and tell story or worse, blackmail. There was only one way to find out.

"What's your game, Jo? I hope you don't think I would ever submit to blackmail. You'll come off second best if you do."

"My! My! Don, Jackie must have really put the poison in. Did she mention that both my ex-husbands sued for divorce because of my adultery?'

Once again, my head was in a spin. Here I am, in a place that was supposed to be an enjoyable exciting experience. Instead, I'm embroiled in a complicated, situation involving two women, one old enough to be my daughter, the other young enough to my granddaughter. If that was not enough, I still wasn't sure just how I was going to conduct tomorrow's event. At that moment, Jo's eyes welled up with tears. It was not long before they fell down her cheeks. Instinctively, I was about to stretch my hand out so as to console her, when Jackie's words – that's the oldest trick in the book – 'most men can't resist a woman's tears'. I must admit, I'm vulnerable in that respect. So what to do? If that was not complicated enough, who should come in to the bar dressed to kill? None other than Jackie. My first thought was how many more dilemmas do I have to endure on this trip? I looked at Jo and inclined my head a few times in Jackie's direction. Jo looked at me with looking forlorn. That did it. I changed position, sat next to her, put my arm around her shoulders. I whispered in her ear, "Forget what I just said, we must unite against the enemy."

Jo laughed nervously. Jackie had seated herself at a table almost directly opposite us. A youngish man approached. They shook hands, then called the waiter over. No sooner, the waiter retuned with their order, when the young man removed from his pocket, what I took to be a mobile phone. At first I was puzzled by the fact he did not put it to his ear. He just held it about head height and panned the area. It struck me this guy must be a reporter or journalist.

"I'm not sure what Jackie is up to. I think we ought to give the impression that we are romantically involved. When I give the word laugh out loudly and look as though we are really enjoying ourselves."

Jo complied with my request. So much so that the other drinkers stopped what they were doing and gazed in our direction. I noticed that Jackie was frowning. The reporter seemed taken aback and quickly replaced his mobile in his pocket.

"Okay, Jo, up we go to my room, are you ready?"

She said yes. So we left the bar. On the way out, I guided Jo toward Jackie's table. As we were passing, I said in a loud voice, "Don't forget we have an early start in the morning. So no larking about! And that goes for you too, young man."

Some of the other customers were still taking an interest in our actions and movements. I'm pleased to say, that was what I had anticipated. As we entered the lift, I thought how nice it would have been if Sandra was with me. Instead of me being further embroiled in a war of the cats.

"I can't possibly spend the night in the same room as Jackie. I'll have to share with you, Donald."

I can't say I was surprised. I pointed out that we'd have to come to a proper arrangement regarding sleeping. As we entered my room, Jo said let's put on some nice music and dance for a while during which time I'll think about an appropriate arrangement. Perhaps it was the cocktails and the situation that made Jo slur her words. I dimmed the lights and whilst embracing, slowly we walked to the window and gazed at the street lights and the moving cars.

"I think I have an idea for sleep arrangements."

Jo's speech was even more slurred. She pulled me toward the bed. She continued speaking.

"This is one of the 'she fell on the bed dragging me with her.'"

It was a bright sunny morning as I struggled out of bed and headed for the shower. Couldn't remember seeing Jo. I supposed she'd gone to the double room for her day clothes. After dressing, I went to the girls' room and was about to knock on the door when the sound of raised voices made me hesitate.

"Gold-digging slut!"

"You're nothing but a conniving Trollope and an easy tart."

It was difficult to determine just who said what. I decided to knock loudly on the door and called out, "Oy you two, time for breakfast. We have an early start remember."

I continued knocking even louder and shouted louder "Open up! Let me in. It's me, Don. Come on."

"We are not ready yet. You'll have to wait."

"I'll wait inside and close my eyes. Let me in please." There was a sound on the other side of the door. Jackie opened it. She was still in her dressing gown.

"What the hell are you playing at? Do you want us get thrown out?" I brushed passed her and called out, "Jo, is everything okay? Where are you?"

"Your night companion is having a shower. You must have over worked her last night."

I stared angrily at Jackie who glared defiantly at me.

This was not the situation I wanted to be in. What I wanted was a clear head so I could focus on a suitable introduction for the day's activities.

So, I had no option but to speak firmly to the two.

'Okay, you two—let's concentrate on the job in hand and leave the catfight till after we've finished. Is that understood?"

Jo was still in the shower and Jackie, looking mollified, turned her back on me and marched over to a chair and sat down avoiding my glance. After what seemed an age, but was only five minutes or so, Jo came in fully dressed and gave me a sweet smile and said, "Don't know about you, but I'm ready for breakfast. Shall we go to that Diner? Her Ladyship can follow on at her leisure."

"Jo, I've already said save the aggro till after we've finished. In the meantime, cut out the sarcasm. That applies to both of you. If you can't be civil towards each other then don't talk to each other. Do I make myself clear?"

I think I got the message home because they both looked startled and uneasy. I decided on a follow up, "I'm waiting for an answer. Did I make myself clear?"

Jo was the first to respond. "Yes, Don. You can rely on me to behave."

"Good, Jackie. Do you understand what I've said?"

"Yes, Mr Donaldson. I do understand English that's why I was appointed by my boss to be your agent."

"Okay, Jo. Let's you and me go for breakfast. Jackie, you do whatever you want."

With that, Jo and I left the hotel and made our way to the Diner. It was such a relief being in the open air. Before we reached the Diner, I asked Jo if she had any ideas about how the event should proceed. Jo didn't say anything for a while. She looked as though she was pondering about something that had caught her vision. I couldn't help but notice how lovely she looked even this early in the morning. Her eyes were exceptionally large. No man could resist the ultimate feminine charm. She turned to face me.

"It might be a good idea if we asked the audience how many of them would like a session on short story techniques. This would give you the chance to have a question and answer session after your presentation."

She paused and I thought this would be the opportunity for me to apologise for the harshness of my reprimand.

"I think that is a great idea. Oh, and by the way, I apologise for my tone of voice this morning. But I'm sure you can understand my feelings."

"Of course, I understand. I'm on your side. Jackie resents me being here because she sees me as an obstacle."

"An obstacle—how do you mean?"

"Come on, Don. You know she fancies you and not just because of your looks. She wants some of your millionaire contract."

Try as I must to focus on the presentation, I kept going over what Jo had just said. Also my guilt feelings about the fantastic night I'd had with her. It was fortunate that the hall was just a few minutes' walk from the Diner. As we entered, we were greeted by the chairman.

"Morning, I'm Lionel, your Chairman Host. As you can see, we are almost full. Should be ready to start in about a quarter of an hour."

There was a large screen set up for a PowerPoint presentation. This was for the benefit of those writers who did not receive a copy of Dilemma. We explained to Lionel that a short story session should be held after the main event. He was happy to go along with it. He agreed.

I looked around to see if Jackie had arrived. Couldn't see her. Lionel raised the mic to his mouth.

"Welcome, fellow writers and to be politically correct, welcome lady writers and those who are undecided which category they fit in to."

This brought howls of laughter and derision. As this was the first time I'd been to the United States, I wasn't at all sure what the 'Public Psyche' was regarding sexual identity. Thought it best not to follow up Lionel's theme.

"It gives me great pleasure to hand over to our bestselling author Donald Donaldson."

I ascended the rostrum amid loud applause.

"Thank you, one and all. After the PowerPoint showing of the best seller Dilemma, there will be a question and answer session and for those of you who are interested in short story techniques, my friend, Jo will conduct it. So, without further ado, here we go with Dilemma.

Chapter Three
Presenting *Dilemma*

Louise, looking into the mirror and brushing her long blonde hair, heaved a sigh of satisfaction. To her great delight, the doctor, to quote his own words said, "The rabbit says yes."

So, at long last her dreams—or at least some of them—were God willing about to come to fruition. Yes, she had married the man of her dreams, well almost, but then again, absolute perfection was not attainable. She remembered the words of her late father (with whom she had a close affection and friendship), "Louise, lass tha'll be dead lucky if you find one who is a hundred per cent right for thee—settle for eighty per cent and spend the rest of your life time working on the rest."

In her mind's eye, or in this case, mind's ear, she could still hear his broad Yorkshire accent. She was convinced that was what made her mother go for him. Mother was from London. Her Southern voice was not lost even after decades of living 'T'up north.

It had been a struggle for her parents but with thrift and hard work, they had somehow brought up three daughters—had lived to see them married off, but sadly did not live to see any grandchildren.

"If it's a boy, I'll name him after your dad and if a girl, she'll take mother's name." Louise always spoke aloud when on her own. For some reason it made her feel happy.

A quick glance at the small, cheap alarm clock told her that there was only about another twenty minutes for getting ready to go out. With a flurry intake of a few sharp breaths, Louise realised she had to decide what to wear. This was always a problem since she married Martin. After all, he is only a man—and what do men know about clothes? It was so different when she was single. Her mother and sisters could be relied upon in matters of this nature.

The restaurant for this evening's outing, The Fantasia, was what she called semi-posh. Not a black tie with a low murmuring clientele—they wouldn't say boo to a goose fraternity, but it was not a raucous, brown-sauce-liberally-poured-over-the-fish & chips- establishment. It was something in between.

Lots of subdued laughter but not overdressed ladies with gentleman wearing smart casual.

Sharon and Jeff suggested The Fantasia because this evening, there would be a Quartet and dancing night. Although Louise loved music and could dance all night if need be, it made choice of what to wear, that little bit more of a problem.

Looking at the Victorian silver framed picture of her parents, Louise said, "Mother, what should I wear for tonight's do?"

"Something medium shade and not too short with a fancy white blouse," she imagined her mother saying.

"You know what, mother, you are right." With that she opened her wardrobe door, gave a quick glance, made a tut-tut and with a sigh thought, if I wear yellow which shoes will match?

"Maroon or grey maybe she asked her mother's photograph?"

"Definitely, not grey," came back her mother's imaginery voice."

"Why not?!!" that was the imagined voice of eldest sister Helen. Now, Helen was always a 'Daddy's girl' who would never miss an opportunity to argue with mother. Not that Helen was in anyway a bad person, perish the thought.

But she had an obstinate streak—no doubt inherited from father. They were two of a kind.

So, whose voice should she pay attention to? After pausing and struggling with the clothes rail, she chose a yellow dress that was flecked with feint maroon stripes. That settled it. The maroon shoes would be a perfect match.

Then, there was the problem of the hat. Should she wear one or not? They would be going by taxi there and back, so why bother.

Then, like a bolt of lightning, it struck her. She had not asked Sharon what she would be wearing. Although on second thoughts, Sharon never wore anything that could be described as fancy. As full time P.A., neat and smart were her watch words. Come to think of it, Louise had never seen Sharon dressed up at all. Thank goodness, The Fantasia could accommodate any dress code. Feeling more relaxed, Louise tried focusing her mind on how Martin would react to the news. When the subject of starting a family came up, he would say, 'If it happens it happens'. Louise interpreted that, to mean he was not on that keen on being a family man.

Martin, a car mechanic, who was more interested in things rather than people, either spent his time reading, or making furniture. Their home was full of his handiwork. Louise was really delighted and happy with her marriage. She smiled at thought and looking at her father's photograph said, "Martin is ninety-five per cent of what I wanted, dad. If he could just be a bit more sociable—like Jeff, he'd be perfect. You see, dad, I've never had to work since I married Martin, so I'm only thinking of what sort of father he will be, if deep down he doesn't want a family.'

Sharron and Jeff were totally different to her and Martin. Jeff and Martin had been friends since early schooldays. Both were into sport and they were good all-rounders in the school's first team cricket eleven. Where they were differed was, Jeff excelled at English and Math—but Martin was keen on woodwork and metal work.

As for Sharon, she was not in any way like Louise. Sharon was tall, elegant with nice long legs. Louise was attractive from the waist up. In fact, it took a fair amount of time, before any rapport could be established between them. Louise felt somewhat intimidated by Sharron. After all, Louise was, as she saw it, just a mere typist in a large pool. The fact that she stopped working shortly after marrying Martin, gave her that edge on Sharron, who although was in a high powered job, had to work in order to live up to her and Jeff's life style.

The arrangement for this evening was that Martin would go with Jeff to his place of work where he would change out of his work clothes and he, Jeff and Sharon would collect Louise.

The shrill tweeting of the phone interrupted Louise's train of thought. A bit early to let her know that the others were on their way. So who could be calling at this time? Both her sisters were away on holiday. With a degree of annoyance, Louise made her way from the dressing table to the bedside phone.

"Hello, who's calling?"

It was a pesky, double glazing outfit. "Not interested!" was her sharp response. She put the receiver down firmly as her face creased up in a sharp grimace.

So, continuing to select the appropriate foundation cream, eye liner, rouge and lipstick, her mood returned to its pre-phone call tranquillity. A thought struck her.

"I'm in the mood for some soothing classical music." With that, she tuned in her small, old transistor radio that she bought, heaven knows how long ago. She was reluctant to throw it out because it had never let her down. In fact, Louise regarded it as an old friend.

It reminded her of a conversation she had overheard between her mother and father. Mother, for years, had tried to encourage dad to give up smoking.

"A cigarette is like a nice companion even when smoking alone." She could never recall her mother's response.

Finally, there was only two more decisions to make. Jewellery and watch. To wear a necklace or not. Not to wear one, she felt would make her look dowdy. On the other hand, a discreet, not too flashy one would enhance her natural beauty. Smiling and laughing as she looked in the mirror and thinking that's the problem with being beautiful, the wrong item would make her appearance look like a disaster.

During adolescence, she would tease her elder sisters with the phrase, 'You've no idea what it is like being beautiful, not just fighting off the boys wanting to bed you down, but there is also knowing what to wear. Sometimes, I envy you plain Jane girls. Life for you must be so much simpler.' The usual reaction was, for one or both of them to throw a cushion at her.

What the real difficulty that faced Louise was, she didn't know just what sort of dance music would be played. If smooch, then a long necklace would be okay. But for Jive and other fast moving dances, it would have to be a choker.

But the problem did not end there. Handbag and watch would have to blend in. Perhaps an attractive Chiffon dress-scarf would be suitable for any type of dance. But then again, fancy pattern or just a plain single colour?

Glancing at the clock and realising that at any moment, Sharron would phone her saying they were on the way, Louise felt a twinge of pressure. Having chosen an appropriate chiffon scarf, she needed more time to consider which watch to wear.

The metal bracelet ones were something of an irritation after a while. The leather strapped ones, although comfortable, were not attractive.

Suddenly, a sharp tapping of the front door knocker made her jump.

"You could have phoned letting me know you were on your…"

By this time, she was at the door.

"You—" she stared at the thick set man wearing a much too large flat cloth cap, "—ave a delivery for Martin Marsden; where do you want it luv?'

"Delivery! Delivery!"—Louise's voice leaped into high shrill mode.

"What do you mean delivery? Now is not the time!"

"Sorry, Madam—this is my last call and I'm already late. Can't take this load of wood back. So where shall I put it?"

By now, Louise had composed herself.

"I'm sorry if I shouted at you. My husband, as usual, said nothing to me about a delivery. Mind you, he hardly says anything to anybody. How much wood is there?"

"A fair bit. Shall I just stack it round the back on the lawn?"

"I suppose that's as good a place as any," Louise replied with a deep sigh.

"Would you sign just here and here?" The man marked his delivery sheet with two crosses. He handed her a pen. Louise signed, forced a smile and said jokingly, "I bet you don't tell your wife anything either."

"Haven't time lass, I'm always on the road. Hardly ever see her so we don't have time to argue."

His raucous laugh put Louise in a much better mood. She closed the door, made her way back upstairs. Looking in the

75

full length mirror and raising her hand and putting her wrist forward, she decided that the watch with the gold plated bracelet would best suit her outfit. Even though it was not easy to read the time. After doing that, the biggest decision of all had to be made. Which handbag? It had to be one of the fancy, just for show ones. At the same time, it had to go with her fancy gloves. Martin could not resist her gloves. There were times when they would throw him into a spasm of sexual frenzy. Come to think of it, the use of the yellowish silk gloves was what started her on the road to pregnancy. So, how apt it would be if she wore them this evening. She imagined the scene. At an appropriate moment, after a dance, when the four of them were seated, waiting for the meal to arrive, she would say "Are you all sitting comfortably?"

She would then, take her gloved hand, take hold of Martin's hand, and turning her head toward Sharron and Jeff, would say, "We are about to become parents." Maybe that sounded too dry and formal. Better, "We are about to become mummy and daddy."

She imagined Sharron and Jeff would receive the news with delight. Jeff would lean across the table and kiss her. Jeff always would take the opportunity to kiss her. She knew deep down, he fancied her, as she him, much to Sharron's annoyance.

Louise still had many doubts about Martin's reaction. Would he go off in a huff making his way to the Gents—because of the shock at knowing he was about to become a father? Or would it be, as she suspected, he simply did not want children. Or maybe, just maybe, she could have been wrong all the time and in reality, he would enjoy having a son. After all, he could teach him how to ride a bike, play football and cricket. But what if it turned out to be a girl? Turning to her dad's photo, she laughed loud. "I'll bet he'll spoil her a lot, just like you spoiled Helen."

Like a flash, she had a brilliant idea. She would say to him, "You know that wood you ordered, which you didn't tell me about, well now you could use it to make a cradle and a cot."

Yes, that was without doubt, the best line of approach. With a final look in the mirror, turning out the dressing table lamp, she made her way downstairs and waited by the hall telephone. Wondering why Sharron had not yet called—they must surely be on their way by now, Louise went in the kitchen, switched on the kettle and placed a tea bag in her favourite mug. As she was just about to pour out the hot water, the phone rang. "Typical!" she blurted out.

As per usual, whenever she wanted to eat or drink, there had to be an interruption. As her father used to say, 'Everything's going right, then up pops Grundy.' She never found out who or what Grundy was.

"Hello, Sharron are you…"

"Yes it's me…"

"Switch on the local TV news, we have problems."

Chapter Four
A Grundy Situation

"Sorry, I don't understand I…"

"Please, Louise—just do as I say," Sharon paused, then in a softer tone continued, "Sorry if I sound harsh but please switch on your telly."

"Well, okay. I'll do that."

Making her way into the back room and picking up the extension phone receiver said, "Right, Sharron. I've just switched—ah yes it..."

The picture of a horrendous vehicle crash and flames leaping skyward, made her gasp, then the voice and face of the reporter came into view.

"So far we can only ascertain that four passengers managed to be rescued and are now on their way to hospital. I am joined now, by Inspector Higgins and fireman John Michaels. First let me ask you, Inspector, what is the latest on this terrible crash?"

"The number 79 bus from Leeds left the bus station on time on its way to Harrogate Central. When it reached Brooklyn Edge, a timber-loaded lorry travelling in the opposite direction for some reason, that as yet we have been unable to ascertain, crashed into it. A fully loaded petrol tanker travelling behind the lorry, ran into the back of it, overturned and all three vehicles landed at the bottom of the ridge. This, in turn, caused a spark—and the result is what we are looking at now."

"Thank you, Inspector. Can I now turn to you, John? Have you and your team managed to put the fire under control?"

"Not entirely, but we are making good progress and I estimate that within the hour it will be totally extinguished."

"Thank you, John. For those of you who have just joined us, the news is that there has been a three vehicle pile-up on the Leeds to Harrogate Central B921 road at Brooklyn Edge. So far, we know that there are only four survivors who have been hospitalised. And we have just heard that the four—all women, are in critical condition but are stable. We will know better in twenty-four hours if they will survive. And now, back to the studio."

"Sharron, are you still there?"

"Yes."

"I'm confused. Jeff and Martin use the 30, so why?"

"Jeff phoned me from the station. There was a massive queue at the 30 something about drivers not turning up, so as the 79 was in and just about to leave, they went for it."

Louise, confused and hoping against hope that somehow he had gotten off the bus before the accident. In her heart of hearts, she knew that it would not have made any sense for them to do so. The only stop before Brooklyn Edge was more than a mile away.

"Have you tried contacting Jeff on his mobile?"

"Sure, but no answer. It just rang and rang and then went dead."

Louise could not understand how Sharron could sound so calm. She always thought she was something of a cold fish. Feeling guilty at her thoughts, she remembered how Sharron and Jeff had been trying for years to have child, and now the news of her pregnancy compounded her guilt feelings. Furthermore, she didn't know if it would be right to tell Sharron her news. Louise needed time to think.

"Oh damn! There's someone at the door, Sharron. Tell you what, I'll phone back in ten minutes or so. Okay?"

"Yes, sure. Oh, by the way, what should we do about The Fantasia? I'll phone them and cancel."

"Of course. Thanks and goodbye."

Then, glancing at the wedding photograph on the mantel piece, her eyes drifted to the Victorian silver frame, just like the one upstairs on the dresser. She recalled the time when Martin bought them.

Then, the shock and doubt of what had happened brought on a flood of tears and a jerking of her throat. Her cries became louder and the jerking gave way to panting. Slowly, calming down and wiping her eyes with the back of her wrist, after what seemed to be an age, she finally composed herself.

Spotting a packet of paper handkerchiefs, taking one and continuing to dab her eyes, she made her way to the kitchen kettle. She had just switched it on when the phone rang.

"Oh hell—What now?" she shouted out just hoping it could be Martin. She walked to the hall phone, slowly with a feeling of trepidation. Perhaps it was Martin, phoning to say he was all right or was it the Police with the news she was dreading? Pausing and trying to control the palpitations, her throat tightening up, she did her best to clear it but too little or no avail. Picking up the receiver, she blurted out sharply, "Yes, who is speaking?"

"Good evening. My name is Colin Kent. Is Martin available?"

To put it mildly, Louise felt sick and dizzy and utterly confused, trying to work out why someone she had never heard of, wanted to speak to Martin at a time like this.

"I'm sorry he is not here and I have no idea where he is." Once again, the tears began flowing and her palpitations gave way to uncontrollable sobbing.

"I'm so sorry. Perhaps I should have explained. Martin and I were in the Air Force together and I lost touch with him after demob. I now work as a bus Inspector and I ran in to Martin on the bus involved in the crash. I gather you must know about that."

He paused waiting for a response from Louise.

"I don't quite understand. My head is spinning."

"The thing is, as soon as I boarded the bus, Martin recognised me and called me over. He introduced me to his friend Jeff and we made arrangements to go for a drink sometime next week. The crash happened not long after I left the bus. So, because we exchanged phone numbers I called you to see if…" his voice trailed off.

"Where are you now, Mr Kent?"

"Colin, please. I take it, you must be Martin's wife, Louise—he showed me a photo of you. He said he never goes anywhere without it. Anyway, I am here at the Leeds Bus Station. As soon as I have any more info, I'll get straight back to you."

"Thank you, Colin. I hope it will be good news." She replaced the receiver. Feeling a little calmer but still confused, she returned to the kitchen and gradually managed to make a cup of tea.

So, after making herself comfortable on the sofa, raised the cup to her lips, sipping somewhat jerkily, she began coughing violently as though she felt guilty of actually enjoying the tea when she should be moaning in despair.

She cried out, "Dad, how do you cope with a Grundy problem?"

"Thar's got to take one step at a time." She imagined his reply.

This seemed to calm her once more and with great effort, managed to finish her tea. Once more, guilt feelings took hold because she was feeling hungry.

It had been lunch time when she last ate and by now they should be at the Fantasia enjoying her favourite meal steak and chips with fried onions. Although, would that type of food be good for the baby?

So now what? Just sitting and waiting was not an option. But what else could she do? Maybe she should call Sharron to see if Colin Kent had phoned her and if so, what extra news did she have? The truth was, even though she had known her for many years, there was no way Louise could share a confidence with her. A real shame. Martin and Jeff were close. Maybe it was because all women regard other females as competitors, so could never enjoy close friendships. Or was that just male propaganda made to make women feel insecure?

Laughing to herself and feeling bad at allowing her mind to dwell on such a trivial matter at a time like this, perhaps a drop of Martin's hard stuff would help her slow down. So getting up, and making her way to the drinks cabinet.

On the way, a 'Will it be bad for the baby?' entered her thoughts.

Of course, baby thoughts would always be on her mind from now on. They would, however, be magnified because of the crash.

Deciding that a little nip would not do any harm, she opened the bottle. Once again, just as Louisa was about to eat or drink, the phone rang. She went to pick it up, then stopped, hand hovering over the receiver, shouting out, "No! damn it! If I'd been on the Loo, I couldn't answer it. So, buns to you phone, I'll have a tot of whiskey and you will just have to wait—so there!"

Walking back to the table, she began to sing 'Let ring let ring let ring.' Slowing down even further, she gradually poured out a somewhat larger than intended tot.

All this time, the phone continued ringing.

"Sorry whoever you are on the other end, I am going to enjoy, yes I said enjoy, this lovely single malt and you will have to be patient till I'm ready to deal with you."

With that, she gave the phone a two-fingered salute. No reaction from the phone. It just carried on ringing as though in defiance. With a sniff and a sip, Louise began drinking. It tasted good. Swirling the glass, and raising it up to the light, she admired its reddish brown colour. After downing the rest of the contents, she dragged a chair next to the telephone table and lifted the receiver.

"Hello, whoever you are. Sorry, you've had to wait so long but I was in, visiting my friend Barron von Tiddlehausen. He lives in the Loo."

"Louise, is that you? If you'll forgive me for saying so, you sound a trifle tipsy."

It was the voice of her elder sister, Mildred, whom she hadn't seen or heard from since her wedding day.

"Well, what if I am, why should you care? And why have you bothered to contact me after all these years?"

"I am calling about the accident, but if you don't want to talk to me I'll hang up."

"Please Mildred, stay on the line. You'll have to forgive me. Anyway, how did you know about my connection with the crash?"

"I have a gentleman friend—purely platonic, I might add, whose brother is a Bus Inspector—the one who knew your Martin in the RAF. And he told us that he had contacted you. So how are coping?"

"Mildred, I'm so sorry if I sounded harsh with you. I know we were never that close when we were younger, believe me, I wish I could put the clock back. Mind you, I was closer to Helen. The age thing you know. So, thank you for calling. The truth is, Mildred, I'm in a real flat spin and that is putting it mildly. You see, this morning, the doctor confirmed that I am two months pregnant and this evening I don't know if Martin is alive or dead."

No sooner had she finished speaking, then an eruption of tears and heavy sobbing.

"Oh, Louise! If there is anything I can do? I don't know what, unless you would like to stay with me for a while. There is a spare bedroom so at least it would be better than you being alone!"

For the first time ever, Louise heard Mildred crying. The offer also was something of a surprise. Mildred also was not happy with her old-fashioned name. Their Father had insisted on it because she had to be named after their father's Grandmother with whom he was very close due to the war years when everyone capable of working, had to work, including their grandmother. They had to do so because great grandmother was there to look after father and his two brothers. In the end, it was decided that Mildred would be named as June Mildred. At school and other places, Mildred's first was called by her first name, but at home, father insisted that we address her as Mildred.

"That's really sweet of you, Mildred, but I think I'd better stay here in case people want to contact me. I'll tell you what though, how would you like to come to my place tomorrow? Say about four and we can have a cream tea like mother used to make when we were young."

"I'd like that so much. I know I'll fetch a jam sponge cake. A new bakery has just opened almost right on my doorstep. So I'll see you then. In the meantime, be strong—love you—bye."

Louise couldn't believe her ears. Mildred said 'Love you.' Louise could not recall any terms of endearment between her and Mildred. What a day this has been! First happy news—then tragic news—and finally a complete surprise.

She went back to the bottle of single malt, and as she was pouring out a large treble and patting her stomach said, 'Sorry baby—Mammy has to sleep tonight—just try and not turn out to be an alcoholic.'

Chapter Five
A Journey to Nowhere

"So, Martin, are you all set for tonight's Fantasia visit?" Jeff himself sounded enthusiastic.

"Can I get you a beer?" He called out striding purposefully to the bar.

"No, I'll have a lime and lemon with a dash of soda. Have got a big job on at the garage. Must keep a clear head."

"Fair enough."

This was their favourite haunt during their working days lunch hour. The Turk's Head made the finest cold meat and pickle sandwiches in the north.

There had been many arguments as to just how old the pub was. Some said four hundred years, others insisted it was five hundred. Jeff and Martin always avoided the arguments. The quality of the food and the ambiance as well as the attractive Barmaids were all that interested them.

"So, how's the world of high finance today? Has anyone made a cool million after taking your expert advice?"

"If my advice was that good, I'd make a million for myself."

They both laughed into their drinks. Martin looking around the salon was pleased to see a number of the regulars leaving. He liked a quieter atmosphere. It counteracted the noise of a large busy garage where he had been working for just over seven years. Jeff, on the other hand, was used to a livelier chatty environment. As an accountant, he did the major part of client contact in various pubs. Often he had to travel around Yorkshire and Lancashire, sometimes even beyond, gathering in the big contracts.

Today, however, because he and Martin and spouses had arranged a night out, it was the Turks Head for lunch.

"So, what's this? A big job? That means you have to stay sober for once?"

"It's a part renewal, vehicle suspension springs and a full re-spray. The problem is, the owner made it up himself so nothing is standard. The electrics need a full check as well."

"Sounds as though the owner is a bit like you, Martin—a DIY mechanic."

"If only he were that good." Martin's face became a wide mischievous grin.

"He is some sort of Admin Clerical type who likes to tinker with cars. He does it to avoid his wife's company. At least, that's what he tells me. You'd be surprised at what they talk about when they bring their motors for repair."

"That's nothing. You should hear what my clients confess over a drink. In fact, one day I'll write a book about it. Mind you, I'd have to use a pen name."

"You know what, Jeff, I've come to the conclusion that you and I are the only faithful husbands in the country. Mind you, I'm not all that sure about you."

An even wider smile creased Martin's face.

"As though the thought had never crossed your mind, you could well be a dark horse."

"As if I ever had the opportunity to flirt. Don't think I'd get much of a response from the big end of a car."

"Must go to the small room—carry on drinking!"

Martin couldn't help but notice the way Jeff inclined his head to the buxom, well-proportioned barmaid standing near the end of the bar. Also, as Jeff turned into the left passageway that lead to the toilets, the Barmaid followed him trying to look discreet, but Martin, a shrewd cookie, as the saying goes, knew instinctively, Jeff was up to something.

A short while later, Jeff returned and said, "Fancy a packet of crisps before we return back to the grind? I'm having cheese and onions."

"Sure, why not? Should keep me going till tonight's shindig."

Jeff made his way to that part of the bar away from the buxom barmaid. As he did so, the barmaid headed for Martin and Jeff's table. She sat down next to Martin and said, "Martin, when are you going to have a look at my big end like you promised?"

By this time, Jeff had returned with the two packets of crisps.

With a smile and a knowing quizzical look, Martin said, "If you two think you are a good comedy act, better not give up your day jobs."

"What are you going on about?" said Jeff, feigning innocence in such a way that it was obvious he was nothing of the sort.

Martin thought he would play along and turning to the barmaid said, "It's my opinion that your big end problem originates under your bonnet on-top, so, that's the first thing I would have to probe."

The barmaid gave a smirk and blushed slightly. Martin added, in a matter of fact tone, "So, if you would care to make an appointment, I can guarantee complete satisfaction."

"Don't you believe him love? He says that to all lady drivers who make regular visits to the garage."

"Must get to the bar, lads. There are some thirsty men waiting and I don't like to disappoint any man. As she made her way back to the bar, she looked over her shoulder, smiled and gave Martin slow wink.

"I hope you control yourself better at the Fantasia this evening. You know your Louise and Sharron never miss a trick."

"Can't make any guarantees. You've no idea what it's like being devastatingly attractive to women. It's something I have learned to live with."

"Time's marching on Martin. Must get back. Oh and don't forget, you're changing at my place."

"All of my things are in a holdall at the garage. So, I'll see you later."

With that, the two friends parted.

It was six in the evening when they met up again.

"There was a very long queue at bus stop. This is no good," said Jeff, "Hang on while I find out if there is a problem."

Soon he returned to Martin.

"A driver has rung in sick and there is a mechanical fault with the bus."

"I see the 79 has just started taking on passengers. Let's take it."

"It's a long way round, Jeff. Don't you think we should wait here and see what happens?"

"I'm not sure. We could be waiting longer here than the journey time on the 79."

"Come to think of it, you could be right and I could do with a sit down."

Soon, Jeff and Martin were seated about halfway down the lower deck. Just as Martin was adjusting himself into a comfortable relaxing position, two women, each with a young child about four years old, seated themselves in the seats in front of them.

Then it began. Turning to face them, one little girl said, pointing to Martin, "You've got hair under your nose, why?"

At first Martin just smiled and closed his eyes.

Turning to her mother, cried out in loud voice. "Mammy that man has got hair under his lip and he won't tell me why."

"Cynthia! Don't be rude, and sit straight. I don't know what they teach at nursery school, but they certainly aren't good manners."

"But I want to know why the man has hair under his nose."

It was then, Jeff decided to intervene. He leaned forward and in a deep, slow voice said, "I know why he has hair under his nose."

"Really?"

The little girl's eyes were wide and staring at Martin.

Jeff continued with an even deeper sinister tone of voice and said, "It's a sigh that he is a child eater. If little girls annoy him, he bites their noses and ears off."

Jeff had hoped that what he had said would quieten the girl down. Instead, she let out a scream, and obviously fully frightened, said, "Mammy, that man is going to eat my ears and nose. Save me."

"Cynthia, keep quiet and stop making all that noise. You are a silly girl. Now sit still and not another word."

At the next bust stop, a number of passengers boarded. As an old lady was passing by on her way to the rear of the salon, the other little girl said to the old lady, "A man is going to bite my friend's ears and nose off because he thinks she is naughty."

"Well, that will teach her to be a good girl and not be naughty."

"I wasn't being naughty." Cynthia then hit her young companion.

"That's enough from you two." This was followed by maternal smacks. Then the tears started to flow. The two embarrassed mothers were unable to placate their off-spring. "When I tell your father just how naughty you have been, you will be in real trouble. Now, stop that snivelling, sit straight and keep quiet. You are annoying the other passengers."

For a short while, all was silent except for the murmuring vibration of the bus's engine.

"Cynthia, no nose!" blurted out the other little girl.

Thinking, 'Here we go again', Martin was just about to feel really angry when the bus pulled up at a stop and an inspector boarded.

Nudging Jeff, Martin said, "I know him. We were in the Air Force together. Wait till he reaches us, we'll have some fun."

As Inspector Colin Kent approached, Martin called out, "Inspector, this bloke, has sneaked on without paying his fare." He pointed at Jeff.

Colin looked puzzled for a brief moment, then said, "I don't see how—wait a second, oh no, it can't be. Of all the buses in all the city, you have to come on to mine. You mischievous, old sod. You are still up to your old tricks Martin."

Then looking at Jeff, he asked, "Is this reprobate with you? If so, be on your guard. He gets up to all sorts."

"You don't have to tell me that, inspector. You should have seen the way he was carrying on with the Barmaid this lunchtime."

"I can well believe it. When we were in Cyprus, the Eoka Terror group threatened to cease operations if he continued larking about."

"When you two comedians have finished maligning my character, I'll ask you, Colin, how long you have been working for the bus company?"

"It so happens, it was sometime after we were demobbed. And this is the first time I am on this route. A lot of sickness and staff holidays meant doing a double shift. Anyway, tomorrow I'm on an extra rest day, which I might say, is well deserved."

"I see you haven't changed either. Just as modest and unassuming as ever."

"So, where are you living these days?"

"My wife and I, and two sons live in Knaresborough. Here, I'll jot down my address and phone number."

He reached in his pocket and held a pocket book and began writing.

"If you and your friend give me your details, we can make arrangement to go for a drink sometime, wife's permission notwithstanding."

Jeff handed Colin a business card and said, "Let's make that drink soon, Colin, I'm Jeff, by the way."

"I see you two live in Harrogate but work in Leeds. Well my local is not that far away and they still use hand pumps."

"Sounds like my sort of place, Colin. what do you say Martin?"

"I'm more of canned or bottled Lager man myself. Mind you, I don't mind lowering my standards to accommodate two good friends."

Colin turned to Jeff, "Has he always been so magnanimous, Jeff?"

"To tell the truth, Colin, I think this is the first time ever."

"Sorry, I can't stay and chat lads. I have two more inspections to do. One on the way to Leeds, then back to Harrogate. I'll be in touch. Cheers!"

By now, the bus was on its way along the approach road to Brooklyn Edge.

"When was the last time you saw Colin?"

"Must be at least six years ago. But as happens with servicemen, although they promise to keep in touch and exchange addresses, time passes and contact is…"

Before Martin could finish his sentence, a sudden sharp swerve by the bus, trying to avoid a loose wheel of an oncoming timber-laden lorry and the collision of a fuel carrying bowser, crashing into the rear of the lorry, instigated a chain of events that would change their lives forever.

The shouts, screams, grinding and explosions threw some of the passengers out of the bus, whilst others remained trapped by the twisted metal and plastics of the bus windows and superstructure.

"What the hell's happening?" Jeff cried out.

"Mammy! Mammy!" The cries of the two little girls screaming above all the other noise.

The bus had more or less split in two. Jeff, Martin, the two girls and their mothers were situated hear the gap.

"Martin, can you move okay?" Jeff's voice straining, heart palpitating and trying desperately trying to move his legs.

"I think I'm okay. It's getting warmer in here. I think it could blow any minute. Can you reach the kids?"

"Just about. How are the women? Can you see them"

"Don't know. Hang on, I can see daylight. There's enough space to get out, one at a time, if we hurry."

"Can you hear us, ladies?" Jeff's loud voice causing a reaction from one of the women.

"Never mind us, please save the kids."

"We'll". With that, the voice tailed off as the lady lapsed, unconscious.

All this time, the smell of smoking charred timber and petrol fumes were clinging to Jeff and Martin's clothes. Jeff by now, managing to orientate himself and pushing his body from off Martin's, tore off his jacket, then wrapping it around his right hand pushed the jagged remains of the smashed bus window. There was enough space for an adult to pass through.

"Can you reach the children, Martin?"

"Just about." Martin's voice was terse, "Come on, little girl, give me your hand. Don't be frightened. "

"Want mammy, mammy, wake up! Please! Please! Mammy, help!"

"I'll help your mammy soon. Just give me your hand, come on, nice and slowly. There you are, that's it. Got it. Now try and stand up. Come on, you can do it."

The little girl, now crying profusely, stretched both arms out. Martin, grabbing her up as Jeff bent forward and lifted her out of the bus.

He shouted to her, "Go over to that long grass patch over there."

Although she did as she was told, she cried out louder.

"I want my mammy! Want mammy!"

Martin, with great effort, managed to stand almost upright. He reached over to the other little girl who was holding her mother.

"Are you all right?" he called over to the lady.

"I don't think I've broken anything, but I'm hurt all over."

"Just pass me your daughter. There is a way out. But, hurry! The smell of petrol is getting worse."

In what seemed like an age, Jeff and Martin managed to lift the two ladies out of the wreckage. Eventually, the six of them were sitting behind a rock on an old tree stump, when the emergencies services arrived.

Then, Jeff and Martin suddenly were seated back in the bus, as though nothing had happened. Martin's reaction was one of total disbelief. He thought 'I must be in hospital; they have given me an anaesthetic.'

Jeff, however, just sat there momentarily bewildered but came to as he saw Martin sitting next to him, "Did the women and children survive, Martin?"

"I don't understand. I don't know. Where exactly are we?!!"

By this time, Martin felt stable enough to look around. Then, staring out of the window, saw a train high in the sky moving slowly on iridescent railway lines. Below the rail track he could see escalators, also iridescent pink, green and violet moving up, down, at various angles and speeds.

"Jeff, can you see what I can see? Look out the window."

Jeff, inclining his gaze in the direction of Martin's outstretched arm, noticed out of the corner of his eye two pretty young girls, probably in their late teens coming quickly towards to the bus. What puzzled him was the way they seemed to be moving, almost as though they were floating. They were dressed in what looked like iridescent pinkish green silk similar to the colours of the surroundings.

They boarded the bus and floated along the gangway, stopping at the seats where an elderly couple were seated just, like there were after boarding the bus at Leeds Station.

Turning to face Martin, he nudged him saying, "What do you make of that?"

Martin, equally bewildered, said, "Maybe, somehow, I don't know how, but I think we are both experiencing the same dream or nightmare. It's just not real."

"Right," said Jeff, "there is only one way to find out."

He stood up and in a loud clear voice, called out, "Excuse me, ladies, but would you please tell us where we are and how long will we be here?"

What followed, made Jeff and Martin feel totally distraught and would remain confusing as time itself seemed to stretch out for ever.

"You can move on your own!!!" This is impossible. Their voices, in unison, sounded like high pitch bells.

Martin turned to Jeff, "Did you hear what I just heard?"

"That depends, what did you hear?"

Before Martin could answer, the two floating females cried out, "We have two non-dead here, the Metatrons have made a mistake."

They kept repeating the phrase, each time on a higher pitch level and volume. The ringing-bell like sound almost deafening Jeff and Martin.

"I'll get to the bottom of this, I've had enough!" Martin's voice was full of determination. He stood up and advancing menacingly towards the females, said, "Oy, you two, just what the hell is going on here?"

"Don't ever mention that word here. You non-dead should not be here. Stay exactly where you are."

Then in an even louder voices, called out, "We have two non-dead. Stop the outer ring, there must be no movement. The Metatrons have caused the problem."

At that moment, from out of nowhere, appeared six men dressed in shining, white armour and carrying extra-long spears, which they pointed menacingly at Jeff and Martin. "Why are you here and what are your names?" their voices, in unison, just like the females, but sounded like deep bass voices of an Opera. It was an understatement of the year to say that Martin and Jeff were lost for words. Perhaps, if possible to say, ultra, totally dumbstruck.

Even so, before they could think of an answer, the bell voices of the females cried out, "They are here because of your mistakes."

Once again, repeating the phrase with higher and higher pitches and volume.

This brought a combined uniform response from the white armoured men. "Not us. Metatrons do not make mistakes."

Although the pitch of their voices remained constant, the volume gradually increased. Finally, it sounded like some sort of macabre duet.

"Jeff, by any chance, is you mobile working?"

"No idea, can't find it. Why?"

"I was thinking, maybe we should contact Louise and Sharron and tell them to cancel the table at the Fantasia."

"You know what I think Martin, before we do anything, you pinch me hard. If I don't feel any pain, I'll know I am dreaming in hospital somewhere. And what's more, I will pinch you and if you don't feel a thing that'll mean I 'm not here with you and I have no idea where you will be."

Martin's mind couldn't take in or work out what Jeff said. So, when Jeff pinched him really long and hard, Martin gave out such a yell, the Knights and females stopped their weird duet.

"That ruddy well hurt, you daft sod!"

He then pinched Jeff so hard and long, it caused some bruising on the back of Jeff's hand.

"Bloody hell, Martin! I didn't hurt you like that."

No sooner had Jeff gotten the words out, when six spears were poised inches away from his face. And the duet of voices bellowed out, "You were told not to say that word here." This was accompanied by horrible, discordant sounds, both bass and treble, of a very loud organ that made Jeff and Martin's bodies vibrate.

"Know what, Jeff? I've had enough of this."

So, saying he moved forward toward the Knights, and in a loud voice and sheer determined manner, looking one of them straight in the eye, bellowed, "If we are not allowed to say that word here, I insist on knowing where exactly are we?

Where is here? Go on, tell me. We must know," Martin maintaining his fixed gaze and tensing his muscles and folded his arms across his chest in defensive mode. Then the music stopped. The singing stopped and for a few seconds all was still and quiet. Martin could feel his heart thumping. Jeff came forward and stood beside him.

"Martin, my old friend. I never knew you had it in you. Well done!"

No sooner had Jeff finished speaking, then the Opera voices began again. But this time, in softer tones.

"They want to know where they are. Do we tell them?" This was followed by tricky little chirping sounds on the organ.

"We must ask the Archangels. We are not allowed to think at that level. Do you all agree?"

The deep voices of the knights had put the question. In reply, the bell like voices of the females pealed out, "If we do, how will we explain that a mistake has been made and who is responsible?"

"You are right," came the knights' response, "Also, they will be angry because the non-dead will have to be returned to earth and there is no known way of knowing how to do this." Their comments were followed by a deep, loud drama type chord from the organ sound.

The females then said, "We must ask advice from more Michaleans."

"We agree, but only if we can call on our Metatron comrades."

"Very well, let it be so."

At first, the gentle whispering sound of rushing autumn leaves attracted Martin and Jeff's attention. Soon, the whispering became louder and louder and from out of nowhere, appeared a host of more white knights followed by myriads of floating females. The groups huddled among themselves while the sweet sounds of string ensemble competed with the organ that played basic chords interspersed with grating discords.

"Know what, Jeff I'm beginning to feel sorry that I asked a simple question. This musical cacophony is driving me potty. How about you?"

"I'm doing my best to remain calm. You know the old saying, 'always keep a cool head in a crisis.' This must be the mother and father of all crises.

The way I'm doing it, is to try and work out which form of emotional reaction would fit into this weird situation. The real problem is not knowing just precisely what the situation is?"

"Good, Jeff, that is without doubt, the best piece of analytical thinking I have ever heard anyone come out with. Were it in my power, I would not hesitate for one moment to award you a Ph.D."

"Thank you, Martin. I feel both humble and proud that my lifelong friend has, at last, acknowledged my flair of genius. Let's hope we will soon be back home and enjoy a first class celebration."

No sooner had they finished their mutual admiration exercise, when a series of new organ chords being played very loud blasted out all other noises. Then, a few moments of silence. All the knights and females faced Martin and Jeff. From the centre of the knights, one of them projected himself way above the rest. Likewise, a female did the same. The knight spoke.

"I, in the name of my comrade Metatrons, have concluded that only our superior Archangel, if not Metatron himself, may answer the question put by the non-dead."

No sooner had he finished speaking, then the projected female spoke, "I, in the name of my Michalean comrades, concur with the findings of the Metatron's spokes angel."

A drum role was then heard. Followed by an organ melody that gradually became fainter and fainter as did the music of a string orchestra. The drum too, became silent. The Metatrons and the Michaleans disappeared.

In their places, appeared a huge oval table. Although pastel colours like the general surroundings, they were somewhat darker. Seated around the table were seven Archangels that appeared to Martin and Jeff as men with various lengths of long, flowing hair and beards. At first, they ignored the two non-dead. From the left and right of the table, approached toward the Archangels, two, tall winged messengers carrying long trumpets, which they blew fanfare style.

Chapter Six
Sisterly Love

Louise gradually emerged from the deep sleep brought on by the whiskey session of last night. Not wanting to open her eyes, hoping against hope that just perhaps the events of yesterday had been a bad dream. No good. Her eyelids fought back and her eyes opened. With deep reluctance, moving the bedclothes and slowly, slowly dragging her legs off the mattress, she maneuvered her way to the toilet. From there to the bathroom. Splashing her face with lukewarm water, she patted her stomach and said, "Promise me, baby, if you do become an alcoholic, you will forgive and try to understand why I had something to make me sleep. You see, you will never know your wonderful daddy. And I'll never see Martin again."

Then, all the events and questions, sorrows and shocks of yesterday hit her memory. The wails and tears came and lasted for what seemed to her, an age.

Finally, when there were no more tears left in her, she returned to the bedroom, drew back the curtains and gazing out on a clear blue Autumn sky, rather guiltily, she felt a trifle happier than of late. How dare she feel even a vestige of happiness after all that had happened? She dare not even think of what the future might hold.

Wait a moment though. This afternoon, Mildred would be coming. There was the house to tidy. After all, one cannot enjoy a cream tea if the rooms are all higgledy piggedly. And the carpets needed sweeping. This brought a few more tears on. That was one job Martin insisted that he, and only he would do. The carpet sweeper was one that he had bought when on a trip to Birmingham. He had been keen to buy a unique chess set which was the reason for his journey. The shop owner also had this special light weight sweeper for sale. Martin negotiated a special price for it and the chessmen, as well as an attractive antique vase.

Louise, now feeling a little queasy and hungry at the same time, whilst trying to work out if the queasy feeling was part of a hangover or because she was about six weeks pregnant. Heading for the kitchen, she decided that a glass of orange juice and a small slice of toast would do for the time being. Sitting at the kitchen table, just about to eat and drink, the phone rang. "Damn and blast!" she shouted out looking at the kitchen ceiling. Another reminder of how Martin would always put the answer phone on before settling down to a meal. A moment's hesitation; then deciding to ignore the phone, she continued sipping the orange juice whilst nibbling at the toast. She did her best to ignore the ringing, but it did not ignore her. So, with a degree of irritation, made her way to the extension in the hallway.

"Louise Marsden, who is that?"

"It's Sharron, I just thought you might want to know, I've checked with the main hospitals. No sign of Jeff or Martin. All the other passengers on the bus have been accounted for." Sharron paused.

"What do you mean accounted for? I don't understand."

"All I can tell you, is what they told me."

"What exactly did they say?" Louise asked. She was feeling agitated and impatient.

Sharron knew that basically Louise did not like her. It took Sharron a great effort just to speak to her. Louise sounded as

102

if she was interrogating her rather than asking in a normal manner.

"I've just said what they told me."

"So, we are not closer to knowing just what's happened to our two? That's not very helpful."

"You could phone the hospitals yourself. Perhaps they may have some fresh info by then."

"Good idea. I might just do that. Anyway, thanks for calling Sharron, bye." Louise replaced the receiver abruptly. As per usual, Sharron was as much use as a chocolate teapot. She could feel a headache coming on. This could only mean one thing, time to get some fresh air. So, back to the bedroom. For once, not too particular about what to wear, she settled for a warm woollen skirt, light weight sweater and short Anorak. Then it struck her. Bound to be a report of the accident in the local morning paper. More than likely with more info than what Sharron said. In fact, there was no point in Sharron phoning her at all. Perhaps, the only reason why she phoned was to show that she was the one who cared about what had happened. Of course, why else did she call so early in the morning? The nasty cow!

The feelings of irritation gave her the strength to move fast and was soon on her way up the street. They only lived about five or six minutes' walk from the local shops, pub and bus stop. That was one of the reasons why Martin chose there as well as the bargain price.

As she approached the newsagents, she read the placard. 'Fatal crash. Twenty dead, four in hospital—two missing.'

"Morning, Mrs Marsden. How are you this fine morning?"

The owner always greeted her with a smile. A kind, gentle elderly gentleman of the old school. He and his late wife had been running the business for well over thirty years until she passed away last year.

"Not good at all. My husband was involved in the crash," she replied picking up a copy of the paper.

"Oh dear. I'm so sorry to hear that. How was he involved?"

"He was on the bus with his friend when it happened."

"Haven't had time to read the report yet. Is he one of the four in hospital?"

The thought hadn't occurred to Louise. She felt a little angrier with Sharron. If she had phoned the hospitals like she said, then why on earth didn't ask for details of the four survivors?

"I'll take a bar of chocolate as well. How much is that?"

"This morning, it's on the house, Mrs Marsden."

"No really, it's..."

"On the house, Mrs Marsden. It's the least I can do."

"You are most kind. Thank you."

Louise left the shop, holding the newspaper and reading it as she moved slowly toward the road crossing. She scammed the columns till her eye rested on the line that read: 'The four passengers in hospital, two young mothers and their two six-year-old daughters are being treated for minor injuries and shock. They are expected to be released sometime tomorrow. Of the twenty-six other passengers, twenty have died and have been identified. Two, male adults have yet to be accounted for...'

Louise could not bear to read any more. All she could do now was continue preparing for this afternoon's tea with Mildred. The alternative was crack up. No way was she going to give in to despair. There was the baby to think of. On reaching home, Louise didn't go in straight away. Despite the chill, she sat on one of the white plastic garden chairs. With affection and a few more tears, she looked slowly at the garden beds. It was not a big garden but the south facing aspect made it easy for flowers and a few vegetables to grow. The only thing that slightly spoiled the appearance, was the pile of wood delivered yesterday. The Hydrangeas were still in bloom even though, a little faded. The Rose of Sharron still had the odd blooms. Blackbirds, Finches, Crows and a single Magpie flew across her field of vision.

Suddenly, a feeling of complete emptiness brought on an even deeper feeling of lethargy. Perhaps, this was nature's way of damping down her emotional distress.

So, sighing deeply, raising herself out of the chair, she headed for the entrance door. Once inside the kitchen, she cried out, "Louise! Pull yourself together. We have a home to tidy up."

So, broom cupboard open, mop and bucket out, and on with the hot water tap. But as usual, whenever Louise decided to do something, the phone would ring.

Louise hurried to the hall extension. Maybe, just maybe it could be good news. Before she could say hello after lifting the receiver, loud musical chimes and a Canary female type voice announced, "HSBC and other Banks have just announced a further extension to the time period for PPI claims. Press 3 for further details or 9 for..."

Furiously, Louise slammed the receiver down and cried out, "Piss off, you daft bastard!" Rushing back into the kitchen, just in time to see the mop bucket overflowing hot water, she quickly turned off the tap and lifted the bucket out of the sink. Putting the furniture into the hall, rushing back into the kitchen, she put the mop into the perforated part of the bucket, gently squeezing the surplus water away. Once again, as the mop head touched the floor, the phone rang again.

Feeling too tired and frustrated to go into anger mode, she shrugged her shoulders and called out, "What the hell—here I go again."

With a gasp, she said, "Hello—Louise Marsden—who's that?"

"Helen here, Louise. We only got back from holiday an hour ago and I've been on the phone with Mildred and she told me the dreadful news. Have you had any further info?"

"Hi, Helen, nothing extra, so far. Did Mildred tell you she is coming over to see me this afternoon? We are going to have a cream tea. I'd be so happy if you could come too."

"We are still unpacking. What time were you thinking?"

"Round about four or so."

"Right, I'll make sure I'll join you. Must get on with the un-packing and tidying up the house. Don't know how it became so untidy during the fortnight we've been away." Anyway, keep your chin up, as they say. See you later. Bye."

"Bye, Helen."

So, back in the kitchen, the floor cleaning operation began. Sometime later, a tired but determined Louise tackled the bathroom and toilet. The mop had never before seen such vigorous action. Thinking that she now deserved a cup of tea, or as Martin would say in these circumstances, NAFFI up! He never quite managed to forget some of his military habits.

How she enjoyed teasing him about them. The thought brought a few tears to her eyes.

Heaving a quite sigh, she switched on the television, took a sip of tea and momentarily closed her eyes.

"So, are you saying professor, just one glass of wine per day can affect the baby's intelligence quotient?"

"That is almost what I am saying because it all depends on the size of the glass. If you take the glass, shown in your clip, it must have been at least half a litre that the pregnant lady was drinking. Not only would it be detrimental to the baby's intelligence, it would not do the mother any good either."

Louise inclined her head toward her stomach and said, "Do you hear that, baby? It is wine that does the damage. The professor didn't say a word about whiskey. But in any case,

106

even if you do not turn out to be a genius, mammy will still love you. Oh boy, will she love you! You have no idea how much."

Before another bout crying, the newscaster was saying, "And now, we return to the terrible accident at Brooklyn Edge."

Turning to face a smaller screen the Anchor woman continued, "Sophie, what news do we have from the hospital?"

"Thank you, Clare. Well the news is, we are expecting the two women and their daughters to be discharged at any moment. As you can see, by the stack of toys, well-wishers have sent to the hospital for the two girls, the public has taken this terrible incident to their hearts."

"But surely, Sophie, the vast number of toys will be far too much for the two girls to use. Has there been any arrangements for their eventual distribution?"

"Well Clare, the Almoner has spoken to the mothers who, although they haven't yet seen the vast number of toys, have said that both the girls are fond of teddy bears, so what will probably happen, is that the two largest ones will be handed to the girls. I must say, the selection of toys in general and teddies in particular is overwhelming. If we adjust our cameras slightly to the left, you'll get some idea of just how many have been sent."

"That is quite an amount, Sophie, do we know... Oh I see behind you Sophie a group nurses and others have just stepped out of the entrance."

"Okay, Clare. I'll just ask this official looking gentleman if we may speak to the ladies. Excuse me, sir. Independent TV North, may we speak to the ladies?"

"You may, but please keep it short. They need to be in their homes as soon as possible."

Slowly the nurses and other hospital staff descended the entrance stairs and a group of TV cameramen edged forward. Also relatives and friends of the now-recovered patients. "Excuse me, I'm Sophie Barnes of Independent TV North. On behalf of us, and I'm sure, our many viewers, I'd just like to say how happy we are that you are once again well after your ordeal."

"We are so relieved to have come through this ordeal and we would like to thank the doctors and nurses and all the medical staff who have attended us."

'If you look behind you to your left, you will see the many toys that our viewers and other well-wishers have sent for your daughters."

Sophie went towards the pile, followed her cameraman. She picked up two large teddies. One was blue—the other yellow.

"What do they call you?"

"I'm Cynthia and this is my friend Jill"

"Okay, now who would like to choose first? Or maybe I should ask you, who likes blue teddy?"

There was no response from either of the two girls.

"Now, I'm sure one of you must like yellow teddy."

Once again no answer. Jill, however, pointing to the pile said, "I like the blue elephant."

This brought a spate of laughter from the adult onlookers.

"You can see, everyone, that being a TV reporter is not always an easy task. What would you like, Cynthia?"

"That orange giraffe looks nice. Can I have him?"

"Of course, you can."

With that, Sophie picked up the Giraffe and handed it to Jill.

"Now, ladies, can I turn to you? I know that you are in hurry to return to your homes, but I'm sure our viewers would like to know just what happened and how you are feeling now?"

"It's all a bit of a haze, really. Suddenly, there was a loud screeching of brakes then a loud bang. The next thing I remember was calling out to the two gentlemen who were sitting just behind us. My friend here, I think fainted, I shouted, "Save the children.""

"So, how did you manage to get out?"

"Not sure. I know the man with the blonde moustache called out to the other man 'Jeff grab the little girl' The next thing, they helped us out of the wreckage. I think they must have carried us away from it. The next thing I remember was waking up in bed in the hospital."

A hospital official then stepped forward. "It's time the patients were on their way home. Thank you everyone."

Louise switching off the telly and flopping back into the chair, could only stare forward with her jaw dropping. A few thoughts competing with each other for her powers of concentration. If Martin and Jeff were able to rescue other passengers by removing them from the wreckage, they must have survived. So, why haven't they contacted her and Sharron? Maybe she should contact Sharron. On second thoughts, better not. Sharron could well have gone to work, just to take her mind off things. In any case, the only ones who may know more would be the police or the bus company. Anyway, the house still had to be made presentable. There was still a lot more to do. So dragging herself upstairs, she began cleaning the bathroom and toilet. She decided after Mildred and Helen had gone, she would have a long, slow, deep foam bath. That should help her get a better night's sleep without visiting the drinks cabinet. So with a great effort, the upstairs cleaning and extra polishing of bedroom furniture, Louise felt a degree of normalcy returning to her. Stopping just for a brief rest, she pondered on which tea set to use.

Usually the plain white was what she and Martin would use. Martin couldn't stand too much frill and fancy as he called it. The fewer colours, the better in our small house he would say.

Today, Saturday however would be special. Mildred, she hadn't seen for years and Helen not all that often because of her two youngsters. An idea struck Louise. Thinking of Helen, she could advise her about baby things. Her eldest, the boy, had just turned seven and her Samantha was only three.

Yes, Helen would be a great help.

The noise of the letter box smacking itself shut distracted Louise from her musings. Slowly, descending the stairs, then bending down to pick up the correspondence, she felt a sharp twinge in her stomach. 'Please baby, not now, no time to rest so behave.' Apart from some advertising leaflets, an envelope from the Gas Board and one from the electricity supplier, made her straighten up with a start. The fuel bills were addressed to Martin, who took care of such matters. Even before they were married, he insisted that it was his responsibility to look after all household's expenses. He also made it clear that she must not go out to work. This was the source of their first serious argument. In the end Martin, with deep reluctance, said that she could only work part time but only if the money would be for her private use and not for family expenses.

It just so happened, there was not the sort of work Louise wanted that was available at that time, so she quite enjoyed spending time at the gym as well as playing Bridge.

The problem now was, should she look at the gas and electricity bills? If Martin, heaven forbid, was no longer alive, she would have to deal with such items. Because they had a joint bank account she was able to examine the periodic statements. From what she could remember from the last one, the account was in a fairly healthy condition. Martin's salary was comparatively high. He was, after all, highly skilled at his job. His boss used to call him 'the man with the golden hands'.

Not only that, Martin used to do a lot of private jobs. He made most of the furniture for the house.

Louise made a mental note to contact the garage on Monday to let them know about the situation. Looking at her watch, she gasped. The downstairs looked an absolute mess. So, with determination, she began operating the carpet sweeper. Soon, it was full and she went outside to empty it into the dustbin. Another surprise. There, by the kitchen door steps, three pints of milk caught her eye. This brought a few more tears to flow. Martin was always first up and he would bring in the milk and eggs.

After a short while, the house looked presentable. So feeling that she had earned a break, she prepared a cup of tea and was about to pour out the hot water, when the phone rang.

'I cannot believe this!' she shouted out, 'I'm sure the kettle and phone are part of a conspiracy to annoy me.' Remembering to slow down and not letting the phone dictate her mood, she continued to mash the tea. Then, slowly walked in to the TV room, sat on the sofa and picked up the receiver. "Louise Marsden, whose calling?"

"Hi, Louise, Sharron here, did you by any chance watch that TV interview with the two women who survived the crash?"

Typical of Sharron. She didn't ask how I am. Just went right in to what she is going to announce.

"Yes, I saw it. Seems our two were quite the heroes. That doesn't help us though—still no sight or sound from them, unless you know something fresh."

"Sorry, not a thing. What I am going to do is find out when they can be declared missing persons. Once that is done, we can legally have access to their money and things like that."

Thinking to herself, 'What a callous, greedy bitch, Louise called upon all her reserves of self-control and through gritted-teeth said, "I'm hoping that they will soon be found," she paused before continuing. If Sharron can be that callous, I can tell her about my pregnancy.

"You see, I forgot to tell you earlier, I am nearly three months pregnant so I am desperate that my child should know his or her father."

A peculiar sound came down the line. Louise couldn't make out what it was.

It was a bit like a slow, growling, sharp intake of breath.

Sharron, not wishing to be outdone in the nasty stakes said, "Oh Louise, how awful for you. Probably having to bring up a child alone. And the child not knowing its father. You have my deepest sympathy."

Louise wasn't prepared to take anymore, "Someone at the door, Sharron. Must go, bye!"

All Louise could think was how and why did a handsome dishy gorgeous hunk of a man like Jeff marry such a horrible, low -down snake like her. I'm sure, with all his talent, he could have chosen any woman.

Realising that all this agitation was taking up time, better spent making some sandwiches for tea, she made a dash for the larder, opened two tins of salmon, spread some margarine on the thinly sliced white bread, chopped up some spring onions and laid them out on the plain white serving tray and finally wrapping them in Cling film. But not before taking two for immediate eating. So once again, kettle on for a fresh cup of tea and putting the answer phone on, she turned on the radio. With classical music in the background, she lay on the sofa with tea and sandwiches and gently closed her eyes.

Chapter Seven
The Way Back

An Archangel stood up. "I have spoken to Metatron himself. He says this matter must be resolved quickly. After a while, laid the blame on the Clerics who have made a mistake in the timelines of the two non-dead. They will have to make corrections as we place the non-dead on the outer ring who will eventually be reborn. Because the mistake is ours, we have to compensate the non-dead by granting them two options. They can keep their personalities or they can ask for special talents, but will lose much of their current personalities. They must each decide now. "

The Archangel faced Martin and Jeff.

"You are now on the outer ring. As I speak, my voice will become fainter and fainter. Decide quickly what you want."

Martin spoke first, "I have always wanted to be a talented musician."

"So be it—but be warned—you will retain flashes of your current memories which may cause problems. Learn to stay calm and live with it. And what about you?". He faced Jeff.

"I'll stay as I am."

Jeff's voice was loud and clear. He thought he was in some sort of hospital and was undergoing an emergency procedure.

The voice of the Archangel had become a loud whisper, "The Clerics will direct you to the best pregnant mother for your return to earth. The Divine symphony corrections will now begin."

The Organ chords blasted out, then became softer. The staccato of a thousand violins followed by the mellow smooth cello sounds gradually became louder.

Whilst all this was going on, Jeff and Martin drifted apart. Jeff called out, "I'll get in touch as soon as all this is over. Wish me luck."

"Same here, my old pal. I'll get in touch with the girls first, you do the same."

By this time, they could no longer see each other. The music became louder then softer. The only difference was, the brass and woodwind were the only ones to be heard. Suddenly the booming of Timpani lone and deep followed by a drum roll that seemed to go on for a long time, then absolute silence and darkness.

"Ladies and gentlemen, your curtain calls have so moved the artists, they would like to perform, if you are agreeable, the finale once again. Are you willing to stop?"

The cheers and applauses and cries of 'Yes! Yes!' filled the auditorium. This went on for about five minutes or so. The audience settled down. The conductor raised his baton. The curtain lifted. The performers took up their positions. As the conductor looked at the leading Tenor for a sign to begin, the lead soprano fell backwards, and luckily one of the chorus caught her. She screamed as a pool of water emanating from under her dress hit the stage.

"Hank, lower the curtain. We have a problem."

The theatre erupted in loud voices. Then the lead Tenor appeared in front of the lowered curtain.

"Ladies and gentlemen! Is there a doctor in the house?"

Three people, two women and a man hurried towards the stage.

The lead soprano, panting and crying, said, "I didn't even know I was pregnant!"

Three doctors barked out orders to all and sundry.

"We need to relax her."

"Ask the orchestra and the audience to sing Happy Birthday—or anything to steady our patient."

The lead Tenor once again came out from behind the curtain. He raised his arms, "Ladies and gentlemen. An unexpected performer had decided to make an uninvited appearance. Our lead Soprano, Maria, is about to give birth. The medics have asked that the Orchestra play Happy Birthday and would you all please join in? Maestro if you please."

With that, the conductor raised his baton, the orchestra played and the conductor turned, facing the audience who responded on mass and the sounds 'Happy Birthday to you— happy birthday to you—happy birthday dear baby—happy birthday to you.' There was a brief pause. The sound of a baby's cry was heard throughout the theatre. The lead tenor appeared and once again called out, "Ladies and gentlemen, our lead soprano Maria has just presented us with a baby boy. Both are doing well. Maestro, the national anthem if you please."

So with the sounds of 'God Bless America', Leroy Washington made his appearance in this world. He used to be known as Martin Marsden.

The return home for Jeff was not that dramatic. His new mother in hospital had gone into labour. A phone call to this effect was relayed to his new father, Sydney Smith.

"That was the hospital. She has gone into labour. ETA one hour or so."

"Shall we drive over now, Sid?" Dennis sounded anxious as was his wont. Always on edge, a nervy type, in no way like the dour, phlegmatic nature of his elder brother, Sid, who was about to become a father for the first time. It was hard to understand how two brothers from the same parents could be so different.

"No, Dennis. I don't let anything interfere with my meals. Especially, my favourite, sausage, egg, beans and chips. You should learn to relax more. Carry on eating yours. No point in letting it go cold."

"Don't understand you, Sid, I should be encouraging you to relax. You're about to become a father."

"I'm not like the usual pacing-up-and-down expectant fathers. That's one thing I learned in the forces—self-control at all times, or as the RSM would put it—self-discipline lads will see you through all emergencies.

Do us a favour Dennis, in the fridge there are two cans of beer. Be a pal, fetch them in here—oh and a couple of glasses as well. When we've downed them—we'll make our way to the hospital."

"You're not going to drive after drinking, Sid?"

"No, of course not. I'll phone for a taxi."

As Dennis made his way to the kitchen, Sid couldn't help thinking, if poor old Dennis ever gets married and becomes an expectant father—the medical staff will need to look after him more than his wife and baby. A pity, he just missed National Service. It would have been the making of him.

The cans of beer open, the two brothers enjoying their drinks. Sid however, enjoying his drink, whilst Dennis just sipping nervously, when the phone rang.

"Hello, Sid. Smith"

"Grange Hospital Mr Smith. Just to let you know, we have detected two heart beats, and to our surprise, you are about to become a father of twins."

"Well, well! Two for the price of one, that's good value."

"Quite so," said the voice laughing, "So it will be more than the anticipated hour delivery time."

"Thanks for letting me know. I'll probably get to the hospital in an hour or so. Bye."

Sid, putting the receiver back in its cradle, looked at Dennis.

"Guess what, you are about to become a double uncle. Tracey has decided that one is not enough, so we are going to have twins. How about that then?"

"Wow! So, have you got all that you need for two babies?"

"What do you mean? Whatever is needed, I'll buy."

The two brothers continued with their meals. Through the dining room window, they could see a beautiful red sunset. The odd cloud drifting by in a light cool breeze.

"Just look at that sky, Dennis. That's what I call beauty."

Dennis inclined his head to look at the view. Yes, it was superb.

He just couldn't understand how Sid could be so calm. It wasn't natural.

"So, what's the time now?" said Sid, glancing at the old eight-day mantel clock sitting in pride of place on the centre of the mantelpiece.

He continued, "Just after eight. So, if I book a taxi for half past, it'll probably take twenty or thirty minutes to reach the hospital and a further ten to reach the maternity ward, which means we shouldn't have to wait long before I become a dad and you become an uncle. So, do me a favour, Dennis, phone for a taxi whilst I go to the smallest room."

"What's the number?"

"Have a look in the front of the letter rack. There is a business card."

Dennis did as he was bid while Sid left the room.

On his return, Sid asked, "manage all right?"

"Yes, but they said it might be twenty minutes or so later. They are having a busier than usual evening. Something to do with a film premier at the Odeon."

"No problem. We might get there just before or just after the births."

"I just can't understand how you can be so, matter of fact and calm Sid. Don't mind telling you, I'm feeling all jittery."

"Dennis, you are a good lad. Your trouble is, you take life much too seriously. You really should learn to take life in its proper perspective. It'll be heaven, help your wife—if you ever find a woman to take you on. By the way, are you dating anyone at the moment? You never mention women at all."

"Truth, is Sid, for some reason women don't find me—what's the word—appealing."

"Look Dennis, brother to brother, tell me honestly. Have you ever been on a serious date? Come on, you can tell me. You know I never blab or repeat anything."

Dennis, looking rather sheepish, blushing slightly and twisting a little in his chair, said, "I did once, ask one of the girls at the supermarket out. She agreed and we went to the cinema."

"So, what happened?"

"What do you mean?" Dennis's voice was a trifle hoarse, suggesting that he was somewhat ashamed.

"What I mean is, did you arrange to go for a drink beforehand? For instance…"

"No, we arranged to meet each other at the entrance."

"Dennis, oh Dennis, why didn't you arrange to call for her at her home and then go by taxi for a drink? So, when you met at the cinema, did you buy any chocolates or maybe some popcorn?"

"No, should I have done that?"

"So, what you are telling me, is that all you did was, sit next to her. So what happened afterwards?"

"I went with her to the bus station and saw her on the bus."

"Don't tell me you didn't see her home."

118

"No, when she got on the bus, she saw some of her friends and said she would see me in the morning back at the supermarket."

"I won't ask what happened the following morning. You certainly blew it big time. I see that I'll have to give you some lessons on how to relate with the opposite sex."

At that moment, the sound of the taxi horn managed to divert their attention away from Dennis's romantic escapade.

"Right, here we go. I'll leave the upstairs landing light on, and the table lamp in the front room. Are we ready then?"

"Ready!"

Just less than a half hour later, the two brothers were in the maternity-ward waiting room. They had just made themselves comfortable when a nurse approached them.

"Mr Sidney Smith?"

"That's me, nurse." Sid's face was beaming.

"Congratulations, you are the father of two healthy twin boys."

"Wow! Can I see my wife now?"

"Yes, but not for long. She needs some rest and she'll probably be here for another day. We need to keep an eye on the twins."

"Why, is there something wrong?"

"No, just routine medical inspection that the Consultants have instigated."

"Is it okay for my brother here to see my wife as well?"

"Sure, as long as he doesn't talk too much."

"I can guarantee it, nurse. He belongs to the 'not-saying-boo-to-a-goose fraternity'.

About a week later, Sid was still making sure that Tracey did not have to lift a finger much to her irritation, possibly brought on by post-natal depression.

Chapter Eight
Jeff is Shocked

"Sid, will you stop fussing so much? I know I mustn't overdo things, but I'm not going to sit around like some useless lump."

"Look, Tracey, you'll have to be patient with me. Ever since Simon had his fits, I've been terribly worried about how it would affect you and…"

"He's all right now. I'm all right now. Lenny is all right now. You are the only one who is full of the jitters. So please, please try and behave normal."

Tracey's tone was loud and sharp. However, she could not help but notice Sid's doleful, sad expression. So in a gentler sounding voice, she added, "I'm sorry Sid, but you don't realise just how irritating it is to have someone hovering all the time."

"I'm sorry, too. Did the doctor say why Simon had the fit? Any idea what caused?"

"No, all he said was that the shock of being born makes most babies cry once they are given the first breath.

He said it could be possible that Simon is bright and the shock is more intense. He couldn't say though for certain what it was."

The truth of the matter was, that Simon, who is fact, Jeff, suddenly realised that he had not been dreaming in hospital and that now he had in fact been reborn. The thought of having to go through potty training and teething and nappy changing sent him into a state of confusion, anger, frustration and for a while, depression. As the early days went by, he enjoyed being breast fed by his new mother. Not only that, he would be able to take advantage of his mature personality. He calmed down and began making plans about how much fun and mischief he could get away with. Also, he could set up his twin brother as the fall guy.

He made a mental note that as soon as possible, he needed to know just where he lived and how far it was from Harrogate. This reminded him of Sharron. Also, where was Martin now? At one point, when he first noticed the three spot birthmark on his left hand, he knew that was where Martin had pinched him. It was that thought that had started the shaking reaction that was identified as a fit. So he had been at the reception to heaven. The angels, Archangels, the music and all that actually happened.

As the days and weeks moved on, Sid and Tracey noticed that Simon was making more progress than Leonard. Simon's favourite trick was to crawl towards the electric sockets and switch things off. The problem was, Simon only did this when Leonard was nearby so more often than not poor old Lenny, as his parents called him, got the blame.

"Lenny, you must not do that. It's naughty and Simon will copy you. So be a good boy and don't touch the switches."

It was about ten months later and Simon was already walking. Lenny tried to emulate him but was always falling over. The antics of Simon plus the fact that Tracey was not a stay at home person, forced her to ask her mother, Doris, to look after the kids while she went out to work, at least part time.

Although, like most grandparents, Doris and Malcolm doted on their grandchildren, they were, to put mildly, a handful. In the end, it was agreed that the twins would be taken to grandma Doris's home Monday, Wednesday and

Friday. By now, Simon was speaking in short sentences—he didn't want anyone to know that he was fluent. Also, at grandma's, there were plenty of newspapers and magazines around which Simon would read while Lenny would sit on grandma's knee whilst they watched television.

The TV room did not have any reading matter in it, so Simon would go into the back room to catch up on the latest news.

One day, an item about Jeff's firm hit the front page. The item read:

'Police called in to investigate irregularities at Willows and Sanford International, the Accountants and Auditors.

A spokesman for the company told the Express that the Landon Margo account was half a million short. Although the Spokesman was not willing to say anymore, the Express understands that the senior Accountant handling the Landon Margo Account was Mr Jeff Fordham who is missing. He was a passenger on the bus involved in the tragic accident at Brooklyn Edge. Just under a year ago. There was no trace of him or his friend who was travelling on the same bus.

Both have been listed as Missing Persons.'

Because there were only four members of Jeff's staff who handled that account, Simon managed to work out who would be the most likely to embezzle the cash. The two youngest, who were studying for their articles had only been with section about a year. So, they were still on a learning curve. Besides, he monitored their work. They simply didn't have the know-how to cover their tracks.

It could only be the other two. Not just one of them. Peter and Jenny, both married, were having an affair. Although they managed to keep it secret from other members of staff, Jeff, always a shrewd observer of what he termed 'The Human Condition', was on to them. Occasionally, when one of them was on leave the other would phone in sick. Also, Jenny would

122

be working on another minor account and would have to work over to meet deadlines. By coincidence, in order to keep the Landon Margo on track, Peter had to work over also on the same evening as Jenny.

'And I thought I could trust them,' thought Simon. He made a mental note that he would have to do something about the situation as soon as he was old enough.

Chapter Nine
The Cream Tea

Louise woke up with a start. Glancing at the clock and knowing there was only about quarter of can hour or so till her sisters arrived, she dashed into the kitchen, and switching on the kettle decided that the earthenware teapot would be best for the occasion. No sooner had she brought it out, then the door chimes sounded. Now, although she had kept in touch with Helen, birthday cards, Christmas cards and the like, until yesterday's phone conversation with Mildred' there had been no contact at all. So, it was a feeling of excitement coupled with a little trepidation that she approached the front door. No matter how she tried not to cry, some tears managed to break through. Opening the door, the sight that greeted her was Mildred dressed only in a fancy, pattered cardigan with a pleated light check matching skirt.

Louise's crying stopped momentarily as the green colour of Mildred's ensemble did not suit her. Mauve would have suited her much better.

"Come in, both of you. You've no know idea how much I've been wanting to see you."

Then the tears and the shaking began.

With kisses, hugs and cuddles in the hallway, Helen called out, "Now then you two, we don't want to crush the Jam Sponge. Where shall I put it, Louise?"

"Go through straight ahead. That's the kitchen."

By this time, Louise had managed to compose herself. Helen took Louise by the hand and lead her into the back room then on to the garden. In a recess, the TV stood defiantly as it commanded attention.

"I do like your garden. Who looks after it?" Mildred gasped. It was an automatic question when admiring a garden. Supposing it was Martin who only looked after it.

Before Louise could answer, the chirpy tone of Helen called out, "Where are you two?"

"In the back room. To your right," Louise called out.

Entering, Helen said, "My, this is cosy. I do like the colour of the suite. Who chose it?"

"Martin made it. We chose the colour together."

"Do you mean he made all of it? The upholstery and everything?"

"Yes. He works wonders with his hands."

"Have you heard anything more, since the accident?"

"No, not so far. I'm expecting a call from the Police at any time."

There was an uncomfortable silence. Helen took the initiative.

"I can't remember the last time we had a cream tea together. It must have been when we were still children. Do you two remember when those three old ladies came to visit mother? I think they were old school friends of grandma's?"

"I remember," said Mildred, "they had this argument about how you should prepare tea. One of them said, 'Tea has to be made in a silver teapot. Otherwise it isn't tea'."

Helen interjected, "That's right, and the other two became right indignant. The grey haired lady said, 'Excuse me, ladies but the only way to make tea, is in a proper China teapot.' Do you remember that time Louise?"

"It's funny you should bring that up now because the third lady jumped in saying, 'I'm sorry, ladies but you are both wrong. The only way to make tea, is in an earthenware teapot. And I must tell you that just before you came, I was debating with myself which teapot to use. I have only two. One is chrome plated and the other earthenware. Have a guess which one have I chosen?'"

Before any response could be made, the phone rang.

"Excuse me, whilst I see who this is."

She picked up the receiver. After a short while, she replaced it.

"That was the police. Do I have a recent photograph of Martin?"

Helen and Mildred looked at each other rather apprehensively.

Mildred said, "Did they say exactly why they wanted it?"

"They think he and his friend Jeff may be suffering from concussion and are wandering around. They are going to publish the photos."

Mildred asked, "You wanted to know which teapot you are going to use.

Well I think, it'll be the earthenware one. That's what mother used to use? I'm no good at quizzes or guessing games, so just to making it interesting, I'll say the chrome-plated one."

"Mildred is right."

"There you are, I said I was no good at quizzes."

They all laughed. As Louise went out to the kitchen, she called out, "Do you remember the other part of the old ladies' argument?"

By now, she was already in the kitchen making the tea. She had left both doors open so that the conversation could continue.

The responses shouted back, "No, not at all."

"Me, neither."

By now, Louise was on the way back carrying a tray with teapot, cups and saucers.

"The argument was about, if you use an earthenware teapot, should you wash it up after use."

Arranging the cups and saucers, she asked, "Any idea how that argument ended?"

"I've no idea. But I can't think it would be healthy. Do they mean, you leave the old tea leaves in the pot and then pile fresh ones on top when you want some more tea?" Helen's voice grew higher in pitch as she was speaking.

"I can't see that being the case," Mildred said smiling. "Eventually, the lid would not fit."

"I think they must mean empty out the old leaves each time. Then, add fresh. But don't wash it up."

"I'll bet it must smell awful after a few years," Mildred shook her head as she spoke.

"I think that's the idea. The old aroma makes the tea more teaified. If there is such a word," said Louise.

"Anyway, I always wash up the pot. Besides, these days everyone uses tea bags. I'm no different. Helen, if you pour, I'll fetch the sandwiches. I take it, you both like Salmon with spring onion."

Helen and Mildred nodded in agreement.

When Louise was safely out of ear shot, Helen said, "It's hard to tell how she's coping with the situation. I hope she doesn't crack up altogether."

"The problem is, she is bound to have mood swings in any case, in her state. Not knowing if Martin is dead or alive really puts the kybosh on it."

The two sisters were now whispering.

"We'll have to find some way to help her."

At that moment, the front door chimes took centre stage. "That'll be the police. Will one of you let them in, please while I go upstairs and dig out a photo?"

Mildred let the policeman and woman in.

"Mrs Marsden is just getting a photograph for you."

"Good afternoon, can we offer you some tea while you wait?"

"Thanks, all the same, but no we have a lot on at the moment and…"

Louise entered the room.

"Here you are. This was taken with his friend Jeff about three weeks ago."

"Thanks very much. You've saved us a trip to see Mrs Fordham. By the way, my colleague, WPC Snaith will liaise with you."

The PWC said, "I hope to contact you once a day or, if you want to ask me anything or if you think of anything that might help, here is my card. If I'm not available, you can leave a message on the answer phone."

"Thank you very much. I hope you have good news for me soon."

The policeman said, "There are about two hundred and fifty thousand missing persons every year in Britain. Most are children who usually turn up within twenty-four hours."

Mildred asked, "And missing adults?"

"A lot depends on personal circumstances. Most of them we manage to track down."

"That's sounds promising," Louise sounded relived.

"Okay, ladies. We'll say good night. Thank you."

"I'll show you to the door."

"Don't know about you, I'm ready for my tea."

Helen tried to sound bright but could only manage a gentle sigh.

As Louise joined them, she asked, " What did you make of that? I keep trying to imagine if Martin and Jeff were concussed, they must have fallen down somewhere and I'm sure by now, someone must have spotted them?"

"From what I've read in the paper, all the other passengers have been positively identified," said Mildred. "That tells me that Martin and his friend must be somewhere else and it can only be a matter of time before they are found. They can't just disappear."

"You know what, you two, I'm ready for the Jam sponge with cream that Mildred has brought."

Helen's face was beaming like a Cheshire cat.

"Come to think of, Helen, you were always ready for sweet things. Even as a young child. I know mother and dad were always going on about sweets ruining our teeth."

"Well, it so happens, that I only have one filling. I make sure I clean my teeth at least twice a day."

There was a slight hint of triumph in Helen's voice.

"I hope you two don't mind me talking about your situation," Mildred said turning to Louise, "but I do think we should try and consider what needs to be done. I am only saying this because the longer we put it off, the harder it'll become to deal with."

There followed a longish silence. The three sisters looking at each other, trying to detect the other two's moods.

"What I mean is, we have to think about our nephew or niece in-waiting."

Mildred forced a smile

Helen, trying to lighten the up the situation, said, "I like the expressions nephew or niece in-waiting. Sounds like somebody about to take up a post in Buckingham Palace."

Tears began flowing down Louise's cheeks.

"It's really very kind of you to support me like this. I don't think I'll ever forget this moment."

"That's enough of the tears, Louise, you'll start me off."

"Tell you what, let's finish our tea, then we can have a serious talk. Are we all agreed?" Mildred's request sounded like a soft command.

"Agreed!" Helen and Louise replied in unison.

"I know. I'll see if there is any decent music on the radio whilst we are eating. I find music of the proper sort helps digestion." Louise's voice had a slight tremble to it. She was still feeling deeply emotional about what Mildred had said. As she switched on the radio, a string quartet playing a Boccherini gavotte.

"I know this one," Helen said, "In junior school, a visiting Quartet played it during a music lesson. We were all allowed to look at the instruments afterwards. I can still remember the highly polished colour of the back of the violin."

The three sisters continued to eat and drink whilst listening intently to the music. By this time, the skies obliged by providing a beautiful multi coloured sunset. After a short while, the twilight gave way to almost total darkness.

"I'll draw the curtains and switch on the side lights."

So saying, Louise carried out her said tasks.

"I'll just do the washing up and make a fresh pot of tea."

"Where are the facilities, as they say in the classics, Louise?"

"Up the stairs, second on the right. First right is the bathroom."

Washing up done. Fresh tea in place. Ablutions completed and the sisters were sitting comfortably.

Mildred decided to take charge.

"This is the way I see the situation. Perhaps it will be longer than we hope for before Martin is back home. In the meantime, bills still have to be paid, etc. etc. So, what we need to know is, just what your financial situation is, Louise?"

"Truth is, I haven't had the inclination to think that far ahead. I've been so upset as you can imagine."

Mildred went to her handbag and pulled out a small note book and pen.

"I'll make a note about what we need to know and do. Have you had a bank statement recently?"

"Might have, but Martin deals with all household accounts."

"What about Martin's salary. Is he due any pay cheque?"

"Haven't been in touch with garage yet."

"Well, all I can suggest at this stage, is go to a solicitor as well as the Citizens' Advice Bureau. I say that because I think Martin is now officially listed as a missing person. You can check that with the policewoman who came here." Mildred, tearing out the page from the notebook, said, "Here, I've jotted down what we've just been talking about. Oh, one thing I did forget, it might be a good idea to have a word with your doctor about the situation."

Helen felt obliged to say something.

"Listen Louise, don't feel too proud to ask me if you are short of money. Jack is a most understanding man, bless him, and I'm pleased to say, although he works all hours—the business is doing well. So, as I say, don't be afraid to ask for help."

"You are both so kind. You've been a great help coming here. I'm not as confused as I was."

With a few more tears and sniffles, she forced a smile.

The three sisters, hugging each other and exchanging kisses, made arrangements to meet up the following Saturday afternoon at Helen and Mark's. Mildred would call for Louise shortly after lunch.

As soon as they left, Louise went in the kitchen. She felt very hungry but had no idea what to eat. Thinking, it must be the baby who was prompting her appetite, she opened the fridge door, couldn't see anything that took her fancy, so the next target was the larder door. Tins of pilchards, sardines and tuna caught her eye, not to mention baked beans. Feeling guilty, she took out a can of beans and tuna. Deep down, she felt that fresh fruit and vegetables were most healthy, especially for the baby. Although she had read somewhere that the baby determined the needs. Thinking that it's a good job baby does not have aristocratic such as smoked salmon, or pâté de foie gras.

Soon, sitting on the sofa, switching on the TV and trying to relax, she was startled by the news item in progress.

"Police investigating the suspected embezzlement case at Willows and Sanford International regarding the investment advisory company Landon Margo, have come up what they term 'a brick wall'. They are anxious to interview Jeff Fordham, who is the Auditor in charge of the Langdon Margo account. Mr Fordham, a passenger on the bus involved in the fatal accident at Brooklyn Edge, has disappeared without trace. And now for the football…"

Switching off the TV, Louise thought maybe she should contact Sharron. She decided against it, because if Jeff's disappearance could be regarded as suspect, how would that reflect on Martin. Her eyes focused on the cocktail cabinet. Raising herself from the sofa and heading for the cabinet, she suddenly stopped. No, this is not going to help. Best thing was to continue eating the tuna and beans and listen to some music. To make sure there would be no interruptions, she put the phone on answer phone. After finishing the food and closing her eyes, she drifted into a light slumber.

A few minutes later, the phone did ring. It was Sharron who sounded angry about the news item and what she was going to do about it. She finished by saying she would call back in the morning. Louise called out loud 'Thank you Lord for the Answer Phone.' So with a feeling of triumph combined with a touch of sadness, she slowly made her way upstairs to the bedroom.

She slept better than she had done recently.

At nine, exactly, Louise opened her eyes. Baby was having a few kicks and she felt slightly nauseous.

"What do you fancy this morning, baby? Cereals, I don't think are on your menu today. How about tea and toast and some cold orange juice? Yes, that's what we will have. And then I'll get in touch with daddy's boss and see what to do about his money."

Making her way to the bathroom, she was distracted by the phone ringing. She was about to return to the bedroom, when remembering that she had not disconnected the answer phone and who would be thoughtless to phone so early? Odds on it, would be selfish Sharron.

So, continuing to wash and dress slowly and easily, she eventually made her way to the kitchen. She was smiling as she prepared the food. Her smile came about because the situation was reminding her of Martin. He would always keep the answer phone on during meal times. Nothing would be allowed to interfere with his food. Louise decided whatever happens, she would enjoy her meals. That was one way she could think of Martin. When she finished, she made her way to the phone and listened to the message. Yes, it was Sharron who asked her to phone back as quickly as possible. It sounded more like an order than a request.

Louise noted that she hadn't said as soon as possible. Oh no—the command from on high was as quickly as possible. 'Well, you cheeky, impudent cow.' thought Louise. 'Perhaps I may condescend to call you after my lunch, late on in the afternoon.'

Deleting the message and glancing at the glass fruit glass bowl sitting in pride of place in the centre of the low sideboard that Martin had made and was his pride and joy, Louise noticed a few Sharron fruit sitting on top of the oranges.

Purposely striding over to the bowl and taking a Sharron fruit in her hand, she shouted, "I wish you were your

133

namesake so I could get double the pleasure of squeezing your guts out and enjoying your taste."

After eating one, she did not feel sated. Again, she called out, "Baby, something tells me, you too, would like to remove Sharron's guts, so here goes Bon apatite."

The second one tasted just as nice as the first. She made a mental note that from now on, each time she would eat a Sharron fruit, it would give her added pleasure of power over Sharron. Louise mused, strange how her irritation with Sharron had put her in such a good mood.

So, with a feeling of triumph she decided it was about time to phone the garage. When she finally got through, the secretary answered. "Can I help you?"

"Louise Marsden here, Martin's wife, is Tom available?"

"I'll put you through, Mrs Marsden. I know Tom has been anxious to talk to you, and may I add, my sympathy for you. I do hope all will turn out okay. Martin got on so well with everybody. I'll put you through now."

"Hello, Louise, I'm so glad you called. I wasn't sure when it would be suitable for me to call under the circumstances."

Thinking how different from Sharron. Tom, a good boss and a gentleman.

"That was really kind and considerate of you, Tom. You see, the day of the crash, it was confirmed that I am pregnant which caused me a lot of mixed feelings, and it has taken me some time to come to terms with the situation."

"Well, that is a turn-up for the book, as they say. Has there been any further developments?"

"Not so far."

"Oh, dear Louise, I don't know how to put this, but I suppose you do realise that with so much work in, I must replace Martin. Not that I'll find anyone quite as skilled. Martin does have hands of gold. So, what I've decided is that in addition to the outstanding pay cheque, I'll forward another three months' salary plus a special bonus for your new baby. I do hope you understand my position. Believe me, it's not easy."

Louise gasped. She had been expecting this is what would happen which was the reason for her phone call. Still, actually hearing the position vocalised, added to her missing Martin.

"I was half expecting something like this, Tom. Anyway, thank you for the baby bonus. I do greatly appreciate it."

"It's the very least I could do, Louise. I'm also sorry that we won't be seeing you and Martin at the Christmas do. Although, if you feel like joining us, you'll be more than welcomed."

"Truth is, Tom, I don't feel like going out at all and in any case, I'd only be a wet blanket."

"One other thing, please let us know when the baby is born. Everyone here, I'm sure, will want to know."

"I'll do that if all goes well. So, good bye for now and thank you."

"Bye, Louise and hang in there."

"I'll do my best."

Louise then thought, better get in touch with the bank. At first, she dialled the phone then quickly replaced the receiver. The best thing would be to go down there, their waiting area has comfortable seating. Also, it would get her out of the house and maybe do some shopping. It was just a short bus ride to the bank. As luck would have it, there were only a few people waiting. Louise was feeling really relaxed sitting in the imitation leather chairs and was in no hurry to be attended to. However, in less than a quarter of an hour, she was called over to the counter. After explaining the position to the clerk, he left the counter and in a short while returned with the assistant manager, who ushered her into a private room.

"We were very sorry to learn of Mr Marsden's involvement in the accident. I don't suppose you've had any more information."

"No, not yet. But the police said they will keep me posted on a daily basis."

"Let's hope they have good news for you very soon. Under the circumstances, the bank can allow you to use your joint current account. However, the two savings accounts that are in Mr Marsden's name only, have to be frozen according to law. I believe, where the whereabouts of a client are not known, the Court assumes Power of Attorney, until such time the matter can be clarified. I have here, a copy of the current account statement for you."

Louise took the statement and noticed that there was only two hundred pounds in the account. She realised that the pay cheques from the garage had not yet reached the bank. Thanking the Assistant Manager for his help, she decided to make her way to the supermarket, which was within reasonable walking distance. The array of all the goods and the different colours cheered her up immensely. The pleasant aroma of the bakery made her feel hungry but feeling a little guilty said, 'Now, now baby—you'll have to wait till we get home.'

So heading for the bakery section, she could hear a man's voice sounding rather agitated.

"How can I work with two staff on holiday, another two rang in sick, and Derek, the doze, as per usual will no doubt turn in late."

Louise noticed he was speaking into his mobile phone. She selected a few bread cakes and a large loaf.

The angry man was standing near the bread slicing machine.

"Could you slice this for me, please?" she asked putting on her best smile.

"Of course, love. Just pass it over."

He passed the cut loaf back to her.

"I don't suppose you fancy a part time job—flexible hours to suit, plus perks?"

Louise wasn't sure if he was joking or not. Perhaps he said because of today's staff shortage.

"If you are serious and we can agree on payment, I would be interested."

The man hesitated then said, "Okay, follow me."

He led her into a very small room, adjacent the bakery. There were two chairs and a desk plus a computer terminal and an in-tray and an Out-tray.

"Just tell me, what work you have done in your very young life?"

"I was Clerk/ Typist in an Insurance firm till I got married and that's about it."

"How do you feel about operating a bread slice machine?"

"Looks fairly easy to me."

"There would be other jobs—nothing heavy—maybe stacking shelves and the like."

"I think I could do that. Oh, I am computer literate as they say."

"So, when could you start?"

"There is one thing you should know, I am just over two months pregnant and mornings are not my best time. I could manage a few hours a day, from say, eleven o 'clock till about four or five."

The man stroked his chin.

"Tell you what. I'll give you a trail. If at any time you are unhappy with us or we are unhappy with you, we'll part company with no hard feelings."

"So, shall I start tomorrow at eleven?"

"That'll be fine."

Handing her an application form, he said, "Fill that in at home. It's not very long or complicated and bring it with you in the morning."

"Okay, thanks very much."

She continued doing a little more shopping then up the stairs to the café. A large salmon sandwich caught her eye as did a cream bun. So with a cafe latte, as well she settled down and looked at the application form. Searching out the rate of pay, she thought it may not be a fortune, but it would certainly pay a few bills. She recalled that a friend who used work here told here as soon as items passed, their sell by date they were offered to members of staff at ridiculously low prices. A whole chicken for just one penny. Stuff they couldn't sell was just thrown out.

The next thing on the agenda was to seek legal advice. She decided that she'll make an appointment this afternoon, and then phone Helen and Mildred to keep them up to date.

Chapter Ten
Leroy Washington Makes His Mark

From the beginning, Leroy, even in his cradle, would coo recognisable musical scales much to his mother's delight. "He must be full of my genes," she would proudly say when husband, Norman, was in earshot.

"I hope he doesn't have any of your genes that will make him waste his time playing Pool and Poker."

"Aw! Come on, lady. Can't a man have a bit of fun in his life? What's wrong with shooting the breeze with his buddies, having drink and the odd game of Poker? Life is hard enough without you going on about what little pleasure I have. Never complained when you are out all the time rehearsing for your next show."

"Of course, you don't complain. The more I'm out of the house, you are free to invite your no good buddies—as you call them—I call them baddies, over here to fill the place with cigar smoke and I can smell the Jack Daniels even before I'm back in the house."

"Now, that's not fair and you know it. Okay, so what's wrong with the occasional cigar and a drop of whatever they bring?"

"This is not the right way to show young Leroy. You are a bad example."

"Me? Me, a bad example? At least, he knows who his father is. Yes, that's right, he knows he has a father. A pity he doesn't know he has a mother."

"And just, what do you mean by that? He knows that we have food in the house and a place to sleep. And what's more, it is a good class home. There isn't any better anywhere in Baltimore. And who is it, who provides all this for Leroy? – Yes, me, his loving mother. What have you ever done for him? Go on, tell me one thing you have ever done for our son?"

By this time, the atmosphere was becoming fraught with danger. Norman knew deep down that everything Maria said was true. It was not just once that she had to find the money to pay off his gambling debts. So, all he could do as in the past, put on his hound dog look and lower his voice into gentle mode. Besides that, he began to feel hungry for a big breakfast.

"Okay Maria, I suppose you are right. If I promise to be better in future, will you forgive me? I do love you so much and little Leroy makes me feel so proud."

"Something tells me that someone is feeling hungry and would like some breakfast. I know all your tricks, Norman Washington. I can read you like a book. And it's not such a good book either."

There followed a gentle silence as they stared into each other's eyes. It was one of those domestic situations, where who would be first to make things better. From past experience, Norman knew that if he were the first, then all would be well.

"I can see we can't have breakfast in this mess. I'll tidy up and use the air freshener to make the place just hunky dory."

"I suppose, you think that makes everything all right. Well, let me tell you, Mr Washington, there's going to be changes around here, big changes."

Norman didn't respond right away but started to clear the cups, glasses and the ash trays from the table.

"What air freshener do you think will be best?"

He tried his best to sound nonchalant.

"You'll not get around me, Mr Washington, with a choice of air freshener. I haven't finished with you yet. And …"

Before she could finish her sentence, the door chimes came to Norman's rescue.

"It's a good job Charlene lives next door and is prepared to look after Leroy. He gets on well with the other three year olds. Mind you, I could do with a few dollars from you. It would help."

Placing his hand in his back pocket, Norman took out a twenty-dollar bill which he handed to Maria.

"That's my winnings from last night's game. It's all yours."

"I'll let Charlene in."

With touch of reluctance, she added, "Thank you."

She tried hard to suppress a smile but didn't quite make it.

"That's okay. Sorry it couldn't have been more."

Maria was opening the door so she didn't have time to make a further comment.

"Come in, Charlene. Leroy is almost ready."

"Right. Morning, Norman. How are you this fine morning?"

"Not too bad, Charlene. Will feel better once I've had some breakfast."

"Take no notice, Charlene. He is not quite out of the dog house, so he'll be lucky if he gets any breakfast at all this morning."

Charlene, laughing, said, "Can't believe Norman is that bad. I must admit, he does seem rather hungry. You can't be that cruel, Maria." Charlene smiled and winked at Maria.

"It's good to know someone appreciates my inner, good qualities."

Norman didn't wait for any more comments from Maria. He made his way into the kitchen and came back with a feather duster and aerosol spray. In a flash, he entered the main room and began flicking the feather duster all over the furniture and walls and in no time at all, began operating the aerosol spray which was a combination of rose petals and lavender aroma.

As Charlene was leaving with Leroy, Norman called out. "Have a nice day, Charlene."

"I'll do my best. My! You are a busy bee. Bye for now."

Mimicking Charlotte, Maria said, "My! My! You are a busy bee. You ought to be given on Oscar for your performance. I'm surprised you knew which end of the aerosol you knew to press."

"Aw, come on, Maria. You must admit I am trying. I would love to taste one of your delicious omelettes. You know, the one with cheese and jam. That's my favourite."

Maria, despite herself could not maintain her angry feelings. Pausing, only to give Norman just a hint of a smile, said, "Norman Washington, I just don't know why I put up with you. It not as though you are a bad man. You're just an idle, no good, pleasure seeking scoundrel. Why I fell in love with you, heaven alone knows."

"An idle, no good, pleasure seeking scoundrel, that's the first time in years you've paid me a compliment. Things are definitely improving. I'll do my best to live up to it."

"Go on, sit down. I'll make breakfast."

During the most enjoyable breakfast, Norman and Maria were managing to have a calm, serious conversation. Something they hadn't done for years. Norman made a mental note that he would make an effort to get a steady job. Although just what. That was another question.

"I know Norman, you have a free spirit who likes excitement and the last thing I would do, is stop you from having some fun out life. But you do see what I mean. Gambling can lead into such trouble. You know deep down, no one ever made a fortune playing Poker. Well, maybe, the odd one."

Norman couldn't recall any time Maria had made such a conciliatory statement and in such a soft tone of voice.

"Tell you what, today, I'll try finding work even if it means just washing dirty dishes in a diner. You are right and I know you don't need to worry about me when you are performing. I have heard, it said that you are among the top five sopranos in the world."

"That's enough of the flattery, Norman I'm not in the mood for…"

Smiling broadly, Norman interjected.

"No, I'm serious, I saw this programme on TV and that's what the critic said. Mind you, I can't say I agree with him."

Somewhat taken aback, Maria said, "Oh! And why not?"

"Because, to me, you will always be my number one."

"I said, I'm not in the mood for that."

"In that case, you'd better get off to rehearsal. I'll wash up the breakfast things."

Getting out of her chair, Maria walked over to Norman and kissed him on the top of his head.

"You find work today and you'll be in for a surprise tonight."

"Maria Washington, I never knew you were that sort of a lady. I am surprised."

Playfully, Maria gently hit him with her serviette.

Later that evening, Norman arrived back first. He was feeling pleased with himself. Not only had he found work, but it was cash in hand, and a free meal a day. The Four Jays Diner displayed a wanted sign for a general helper. Not only that, he started right away. The name Four Jays stood for: Jolly Juggling Jack Joker. Jolly Jack used to be a circus performer until he had a major accident. Most of the time he would sit on a high stool doing light jobs and keeping an eye on the

143

workers. He used all his savings to buy the Diner that had recently opened.

Norman liked the idea that he would be paid by the hour. The longer he worked, the more money he earned. So what if it was boring. At least different people would be coming in. Jolly Jack told him there were, so far, only three regulars.

No sooner had Norman finished washing and shaving when Maria returned.

"I'm so whacked! The new Baritone is not to my liking. He has no idea how to act. The other girls are not too keen either. Well, tell me did you manage to find work?"

"Not only did I find work, I have just had my first day's pay."

Maria, with a quizzical look, asked, "What do you mean?"

"Simple. I work at the Four Jays Diner. I'm paid by the hour, cash in hand. The boss does that, so if anyone doesn't suit, he fires them on the spot."

Maria knew very well that was how the low class catering trade operated.

She had a job like that when working her way through college.

Walking towards him, she opened her arms, smiling said, "Come here, you gorgeous hunk."

Norman did not hesitate. In an instant, they were locked in a passionate embrace.

"I do hope you don't get too bored with the job."

"Well, if this is what I can expect each time I finish work, it'll be worth all the boredom in the world."

As they stepped away from each other, the sound of the door chimes diverted their attention.

"That'll be Charlene with Leroy."

Maria moved toward the door at a leisurely pace and had barely opened it when Tony, Charlotte's husband, stepped in and crying out, "Come over to my place now, you two. You've got to see this! It's amazing!"

"Is something wrong? What's happening?"

"No, nothing's wrong. Just come now, both of you. This is sensational."

Looking at each other in blank surprise, Norman and Maria stood still momentarily.

"Come on, it's okay." Tony was most insistent.

"You go ahead, Maria, I'll lock up. Can't be too careful."

When Norman reached Tony and Charlotte's place, he could hear playing some Gershwin melodies on the music centre. Maria, Tony and Charlotte were standing, mouths open wide as Leroy, sitting at a keyboard was accompanying the music. Tony beckoned Maria and Norman over to him

"I bought this last night and fixed it up this morning. Charlotte told me that this morning she would teach the kids to sing 'Daisy'. As soon as she started singing, your Leroy climbed on the stool and joined in."

"He often used to try harmonise with me even when he was just two.

Told you he had my genes." Maria's voice was barely a whisper.

Charlotte came over.

"He's been playing all afternoon. Some tunes I didn't recognise, but they were definitely proper melodies."

"You mean, he could be composing as well?" Norman blurted out.

"The thing is, he hasn't had any lunch and I'm sure he must be hungry."

Maria decided she must take charge.

"Leroy, stop playing now. We must go home and have some supper."

"Why, mom? I'm happy here."

"Leroy, aunt Charlotte and uncle Tony want their supper too. You'll come back tomorrow if you are a good boy."

Leroy, with grumpy expression and looking glum, came off the stool.

Norman took Leroy's hand.

"Say good night and thank you, Leroy."

Looking at the floor, sulking, he said, "Good night all and thank you."

Back at home, Norman and Maria began discussing whether to let Leroy play on their piano. Till now, the piano was out of bounds to Leroy. On the whole, he was what most parents would term, a good child. The only real problem was the recurrent nightmare.

"What's he doing now?" Maria asked Norman.

"I think he is in the music room, looking at the piano."

"I know someone who would like fried egg with French fries followed by ice cream."

Maria made sure her voice was loud enough to carry as far as the music room.

In came Leroy, smiling.

"With ice cream?"

"Yes, Maestro, with a choice of flavours."

"Can I play the piano before eating?"

"Okay, but after supper, you go straight to bed and get a good night's rest."

"Can I listen to radio music in bed?"

Maria looked at Norman, who said, "I think if Leroy is a good boy, we should let him listen for a whole half-hour."

"Yippee!" shouted Leroy, heading for the piano.

A few moments later, the sound of Beethoven's Moonlight Sonata resounded through the house.

About an hour later, with Leroy in bed, listening to the night's best classical pieces, Norman and Maria were for once, without TV entertainment.

Norman, opening the conversation, remarked, "It's a good job we don't have any drums in the house."

"The question is, how and what do we do?"

"I suppose a good music teacher is a must. We can't let that talent go to waste and…"

"Norman, I almost forgot. Tomorrow, at eight sharp, Top Line TV is coming to interview me. It's their early morning breakfast show. They want to talk about the new production of Carmen. The thing is, Leroy is always up between six and seven. Who knows what he might get up to? Not only that, I need to be at Four Jays before eight because that's when it's busy breakfast time. So, will you be able to cope with our boy wonder and a TV interview?"

"Suppose I'll have to."

"But, as I was saying, we need a good music teacher, and they cost money."

Norman paused and a smile gradually widened on his face till it was beaming.

"Maria I've just had a great idea. What do you think if during your interview, Leroy could be playing the piano, he would as they, say steal the show? You would be asked how you cope with an infant genius."

"Now, hold it right there, Norman. I don't want my son turned into a freak show."

"You've got me all wrong. Once Leroy has the publicity, all the Music colleges will be competing to have him as one of their pupils. And what about the food commercials?"

"Food commercials? I don't follow you."

"It'll go like this or something similar. 'What does the mother of a child-musical-genius give him for breakfast? The well-known, Soprano, Maria Washington says. 'You can't go wrong with 'Brekko cereals' or something like that. The fees would pay for the tuition costs."

Norman noticed the deep frown on Maria's face. She was about to say something when Norman forestalled her, "I know how you might feel about the ethics of exploitation of the young, so if you don't feel it would be right, then okay. All I'm saying is, just think about it. If needs be, I could work double shift that would certainly be a help with the tuition fees."

Norman made sure that his hound dog sad expression was the best he could muster.

"Norman Washington, don't try that expression to get your own way.

It's not going to work this time."

"I don't know what you mean. I've only said what the two possible alternatives are. Maybe you have thought of something I've missed. In any case, whatever you decide is fine with me."

"Norman, you are such a crafty manipulator. You don't deceive me for one second."

Norman made a mental note. She called him 'Norman', not 'Norman Washington'. Or just 'Mr Washington'. "Deception! I don't know what you mean. All I said in some many words is, I'll go along with whatever you decide."

"You know perfectly well I'd never go along with you working double shifts. I know I said you should get a job. But double shift working is not a proper life."

"In that case, let's try and think of another way to pay for tuition fees. If the only way for our son to get what he needs means that I have to wash dishes all day and night, then I'm prepared to do so."

"Oh, Norman. I'm not sure whether I liked you better as a poker, pool-playing, smoking and drinking no goodnik, or hard done by wage slave."

"Jokes apart Maria. Some way or another, we must find a way for tuition fees. Or maybe, we should leave it on fate and carry on as we are. You're right when you say you don't relish the idea of me working night and day. I'm not happy about it myself. Anyway, let's see if there is something worthwhile on TV. It'll give us both a chance to see if we can come up with fresh ideas."

During the night, after the TV had finally driven them to bed, Norman woke with a start. The noise from Leroy's bedroom meant he was having another nightmare. So, tiptoeing carefully, so as not to wake Maria, he entered Leroy's room. Before picking Leroy up, he heard him say "Jeff! Jeff! Must save the girls! Hurry! Hurry!"

"Now, now Maestro, it's all right. You are home with mom and dad. Everything is all right."

Gently swaying to and fro for a short while, he then placed Leroy back in his bed. It was almost the same words Leroy shouted out in his nightmares. The name Jeff and the girls were always called for. Sometimes he mentioned the outer ring stopping. It was all very puzzling. Perhaps his musical genius had a down side. A supersensitive brain also.

Should they take him to a doctor? Medical fees were not cheap. Everything boiled down to money. Settling down in bed, Norman reflected on the circumstances of Leroy's birth. Maria had no idea she was pregnant. They always took the right precautions. Did that mean he was not the father? How could that be? Leroy's resemblance to him was quite easy for anyone to see. But something was not right. As he tried turning it over and over in his mind, he nodded off, only to be awoken by the radio alarm. He gave Maria a nudge.

"Time to get up, sleepy-head. Must dash, I'm needed at Four Jays. See you tonight. Have a good day."

The usual semi-groan combined with 'yeah, yeah okay. Bye' sent him on his way to the bathroom. On the way back, he called in Leroy's room. He was wide awake. He smiled at Norman.

"Are you okay, Maestro?"

Leroy just smiled and giggled.

"Bye, son. See you tonight."

"Good morning, Baltimore. This morning this is Top Line TV breakfast. I'm your hostess for today. My name is Bernice Day and today we are in the home of Baltimore's top soprano, Maria Washington."

"Come now, Bernice, there are many fine opera singers in Baltimore. I'm just one of the many good sopranos."

"Modest, as always, Maria. Tell me, how do you manage to be a mother and follow a demanding career, with rehearsals and practicing, as well as looking after a three-year-old infant?"

"I don't mind telling you it took a while adapting to motherhood. You probably recall, Leroy decided to make a dramatic entrance into this world just after a performance ended at the local theatre."

"Yes indeed. I was there that night. So, how come you had no idea that you were pregnant?"

"The doctors say that this sort of pregnancy does occur from time to time. I was told, on average, throughout the world, it occurs once every two years or so."

"I must say I had no idea about—is that young Leroy just coming into the room?"

Bernice signalled to the cameraman to focus on Leroy.

"I see he is making his way to the piano. Can he play anything yet?"

"I won't comment, Bernice, just listen."

Leroy went straight away in to the Moonlight Sonata. The cameraman moved closer to Leroy.

The cameraman signalled to Bernice and Maria to stand by the piano.

"How long has Leroy been taking lessons? Who is the teacher who taught him? This truly is a first for Baltimore."

"He hasn't had any lessons. The first time Leroy touched a keyboard of any type was yesterday."

"And where was this?"

"Next door. My neighbour, Charlotte, runs a nursery where I leave Leroy. Her husband, Tony bought a keyboard yesterday. Charlotte told me that as soon as it was in position, Leroy started playing 'Daisy Belle', the song that Charlotte had taught the class earlier."

"Would you mind if I had a few words with Leroy?"

"Fine, go ahead."

"Hello, Leroy. Can you play something else for us?"

Leroy smiled and played a melody with gusto. When he finished, Bernice turned to the camera.

"Well, folks. What do you make of that? If there is anyone out there who recognises the last tune Leroy played, please get in touch with me at Top Line TV. Thank you all for watching and thank you Maria Washington and not forgetting, young maestro, Leroy Washington. It's back to the studio."

Chapter Eleven
Jeff Strikes Back

Louise, by now, was coming to terms with the strong possibility that Martin and Jeff were dead. Although each time she thought of the words death and dead, it sent a mild shiver through her body. The baby was due in about two weeks and she had to give up work at the supermarket. She was sorry about that because she'd made a few friends, not to mention the giveaway prices of the out-of-sell by date's products. Just fancy—a whole chicken for just one penny.

The visit to the solicitors made sombre listening. Missing persons' legislations differed in England and Wales to what it was in Scotland and Northern Ireland. It all boiled down to whether presumption of death after seven years was part of Common Law or need there be statutory legislation needed by Parliament.

The domestic bills—Water, gas, electric and council tax still had to be paid. Their argument was, their supplies were, to the property not to an individual person, therefore, bills must be met.

The bank showed some understanding and offered her a long-term loan which she had no option but to accept.

Then out of the blue, watching a TV comedy, the phone rang. For most of the time, Louise kept the answer phone on: then if it was someone she didn't want to speak to—or some irritating salesperson, she could ignore it. For some reason she'd forgotten to switch it on this evening. It was right in the middle of a good part of the comedy. She waited a longish while before raising the receiver, hoping whoever it was would become impatient and ring off. This was not the case. The thought that it could be Sharron wanting to give her an earful, caused a lot of discomfort. The ringing did not cease.

There was no alternative, so with a feeling of trepidation, she lifted the receiver and putting on a weak doleful voice said, "Hello, Louise Marsden here, who's speaking please?"

"It's me, Sharron, you took a long-time answering. Are you okay?"

Pulling a face at the phone and thinking what a nasty sod Sharron was, replied, "Sorry about that, I was in the loo. We had intended to have a phone extension there but before we couldn't come to a decision since Martin disappeared. Also in my condition, I've only two weeks or so to go before the baby is due, so I couldn't suddenly dash out to answer the phone."

Louise got much pleasure in reminding Sharron who was capable of bearing children and who not.

"Right, well, listen up. I've managed to appear on television. There's a programme that deals with social problems and I contacted them. I said that we would like to take part. They will pay expenses. It's next Sunday. So, I've booked a taxi and it will come to me first then we'll call for you at eight sharp."

Louise, hackles rising at the cheeky impudence said, "I do wish you would have asked me first. It so happens, I've made other arrangements for Sunday and I have no desire to appear on TV."

"I'm sorry you feel that way. You do know what they are saying in the Sunday papers about Jeff and Martin's disappearance."

"I've no idea and what's more, I can't be bothered to read any Sunday scandal rag. My doctor says that in my condition,

I should remain relaxed as much as possible and not let anything upset me."

"Well, that's as maybe. I'm not having any mud slung at my Jeff. Don't you feel any sense of loyalty to Martin?"

"Sharron, I don't like your attitude. If you'd paid attention to what I've just said, you'd know I don't know what you are talking about. I repeat, I do not read the Sunday papers."

"Well, if you did, you'd know that they are implying that Jeff was behind the half million embezzlement at his firm and that Martin was also somehow involved. I intend to give them hell on the TV programme. If you don't care what is said about Martin, it doesn't say much for you."

"And if you were capable of having children, you'd know that my concern now is for the health of my baby." Louise felt some regret for having said that. But the way bossy Sharron had spoken to her was more than she could bare. She could not contain herself.

'That was totally uncalled for, Louise. I can see I am wasting my time talking to you."

"In that case, good bye."

Louise, calling upon all her powers of self-control, replaced the receiver gently. She switched on the answer phone and headed for the kitchen. It was obvious why Sharron wanted her to participate in the programme. It would be back-up for her. Thinking that relaxation was what she had to concentrate on, it was kettle on and right to the chocolate biscuits. Looking out of the window, a bright full moon bathed the back lawn in a silvery light. Admiring the beauty of the night sky, Louise went upstairs and took out from the bedroom wardrobe, a long warm coat. The only way to get Sharron out of her mind was to walk round the back garden and gaze up at the stars of Orion and those others she didn't know the names of. It was indeed a beautiful night. Sometimes, she and Martin would take pairs of binoculars and he would point out some of the planets.

Descending the stairs, she could hear the phone ringing. Its odds on that'll be Sharron again. Although Louise was tempted to listen to the answer phone, she thought the better of it, and decided to remain outside. The cold night air made her feel in the pockets of the coat and thank goodness a pair of fur lined gloves were there. Taking deep breaths and walking slowly, her thoughts turned to Martin. Although, like most couples, they had their arguments, but they were never vicious. Martin was always ready to compromise. Perhaps now it was up to her to compromise with Sharron. But she was so insufferable. So, drinking her tea and munching a chocolate biscuit, she went back into the house.

Removing her coat and slinging it over a chair, she sat comfortably on the sofa and listened to the answer phone message. Yes, it was Sharron.

"Sharron here. I'm sorry, Louise, if I upset you. I do feel if you were in possession of all the facts about the slurs and innuendoes in the press article, you would feel as I do that Jeff and Martin's good names and reputation should be defended. Please, phone me back. I don't want our long friendship to end. Bye."

Louise could only gasp and burst out laughing. Long friendship!! What long friendship? Martin and Jeff were long-standing friends. She and Sharron were just two appendages. Perhaps publicity about their situation would put pressure on the powers that be and with public opinion on their side, some form of financial help might be forthcoming.

Louise dialled Sharron's number. She wondered if Sharron would let it ring a long time as she did when Sharron called her. On second thoughts, perhaps it would be too unkind to harbour such a judgmental approach. To Louise's surprise, Sharron picked up straight away.

"Is that you Louise? Sorry about our cross words. I suppose we've both been a bit tetchy of late, and who could blame us? The trouble I've had with the bank. No doubt, you have had it too. I can't have any access to Jeff's accounts even the one from which he paid all the bills. They said legally because Jeff is listed as a missing person, the courts have power of attorney which means his accounts are frozen."

"I know how it is, Sharron. Martin's savings accounts are untouchable and I have absolutely no idea what's in them. I was forced to take out a bank loan, which meant, I must go out to work for the first time in years. I was so exhausted by the time I got home, I just wanted to flop down and fall asleep, which I couldn't so easily because of the baby kicking and feeling hungry."

In conciliatory tone, Sharon said, "I can understand why the TV show on Sunday wouldn't be something you'd fancy. I just thought maybe the publicity could help us."

"You know what, Sharron; I must admit there is something in what you say. How about you come around in the taxi as planned and if I feel up to it, I'll go with you. Is that okay with you?"

"That's great, Louise. I'll do that and once again apologies for the way I shouted at you before."

"As the old saying goes, 'least said, soonest mended.'"

"You're so right, Louise. Oh, and by the way, after our TV debut, would you like to come to my place for a spot of lunch?"

"Sharron that would be so nice. It'll bring back fond memories of how Jeff and Martin would sit there engrossed in a game of chess and we would criticise what was on the telly. I do wish those days were back again. It is such a pity we didn't appreciate it at the time."

At that moment, Louise burst into tears. She could hear sobs at the other end of the line.

"Louise, you've no idea how much I think of those times. I think about them at least once every day."

"Anyway, Sharron. I'll do my best to be ready for Sunday."

"Right, Louise. Bye, for now."

"Bye, Sharron."

Louise woke early Sunday morning. As if the fates were with her, there was no morning sickness and she managed a reasonable breakfast. A general consensus of opinion would be that she was carrying the baby well. Her front did protrude as far as she thought it might. Her regular check-ups did not show any signs of any irregularities. And what a thrill it was to hear the baby's heartbeat. Helen and Mildred took it in turns to visit her every few days. They both gave her some cash. It was, as they put it, something for the baby-account, when he arrived.

A toot on the taxi horn. Louise, drawing the curtain back and giving a wave. So, door locked, Windows checked. All okay and off to the TV studios.

"Good Morning one and all. This morning we are looking at the way relatives of missing persons' cope, that is, if they can cope at all. It is startling to know that on average, more than a quarter of a million people in Britain alone, go missing every year. Until our team of researchers found this out, I had not a clue about this problem. Everyone in the audience has been involved with missing persons. On the panel, we have, from left to right, Mrs Sharron Fordham and sitting next to her is Mrs Louise Marsden. Both their husbands, two close friends, were travelling on the bus that was involved in the Brooklyn Edge tragic pile up.

Also on the panel, is Conrad Green, editor of the Sunday Clarion and next to him we have professor Julian Marks, Chief Engineer of the Mechanical and Electrical Engineering Institute. Let me first turn to you, Sharron Fordham, I know

157

you were very keen to participate in today's show. Please tell us why."

Sharron made sure that her skirt was hitched high enough to reveal her shapely legs. This is a trick all female presenters do.

"My reasons are two-fold. It is horrendous enough not knowing whether my husband is alive or dead, but have his reputation maligned by a trashy, scandal-sheet like the Sunday Clarion is too much to bear and is totally unacceptable."

"Just let me interrupt you for one second. Conrad Green, is your paper nothing more than a trashy, scandal-sheet?"

"I do not recognise such a description of my highly informative and entertaining newspaper."

To the cries of 'rubbish' from the audience, as well as, 'What a load of tosh', the presenter waived his hand and asked for quiet.

"Sharron, would you like to make further comments?"

"Not only does this trashy scandal sheet distort news, it makes things up as it goes along. According to last week's edition, my husband and my friend's husband somehow managed to cause the Brooklyn Edge accident so they could disappear and make off with half a million pounds of embezzled money from Langdon Margo."

"Forgive me, for interrupting but I cannot allow such slanderous attack on my newspaper. I demand an immediate apology from the lady."

"An apology he will never get. Have here, is a copy of last week's edition. May I read the passage in question?"

"Please, do."

"It reads: The Police investigation is still no nearer to finding out just who is responsible for embezzling more than a half a million pounds from the Langford Margo account handled by Willows and Sanford International. They have stated they are anxious to interview the chief auditor of the account, Mr Jeff Fordham, who somehow managed to leave the site of the Brooklyn Edge traffic accident. Twenty people lost their lives in that tragic pile up. Four passengers, two women and their young daughters as well as the drivers of the three vehicles were hospitalised. The only two passengers who probably survived but whose whereabouts are unknown, were Mr Jeff Fordham and his close friend, Mr Martin Marsden.

Now, if that article is not a slur on my husband's reputation and that of his friend, I don't know what is."

Rapturous applause emanated from the audience.

"Chairman, may I respond to the lady's scurrilous accusations?"

"For the moment, no. At this point, I would like to hear from Mrs Louise Marsden. Mrs Marsden, as we all know, your husband, a passenger on the bus is listed as a missing person. Please tell us how this has affected your life."

Louise cleared her throat.

"On the day the accident happened, the four of us Sharron, Jeff and Martin had arranged a night out. We were going to a place where we could enjoy dancing and a meal. I wanted to surprise Martin with the news that earlier that morning, the doctor confirmed that I was pregnant."

At this point, Louise paused to take a sip of water and Sharron left her seat and put an arm around her. There were loud gasps from the audience.

The presenter asked, "By any chance is this your first pregnancy?"

Louise nodded and wiped away a tear. Someone in the audience shouted out, "Close down that nasty scandal rag, The Sunday Clarion."

This was followed by cries of 'Here! Here! And 'the sooner the better.'

"May I please ask for order, whilst Mrs Marsden is speaking? I know the viewing public will be keen to know a lot more. Please continue, Mrs Marsden."

"Since that time, I've had to find work in order to make ends meet. The law does not permit me to use my husband's savings accounts. All in all, it has been a rather harrowing time."

"Thank you, Mrs Marsden. By the way, if it is not too personal a question, when is the baby due?"

"Any time now. Probably next Tuesday or Wednesday."

Indiscernible murmurings from the audience followed.

"Perhaps Mr Green, you would like to justify the comments in last Sunday's edition?"

"Yes, chairman, I would like to ask Mrs Fordham, which words in the article imply improper behaviour against your husband and his friend?"

Sharron, in a most dramatic manner, with a slight tremor in her voice, and looking around the audience, began, "The words 'probably survived' and 'the police wish to interview Mr Fordham the chief auditor'. The way this article is presented clearly accuses my husband of being an embezzler. Furthermore, the words 'probably survived' implies they believe he is dead. How do I know this? Because law does allow anyone to say what they like or write what they like about a dead person? Because the legal status of my husband and his friend is in doubt, it is no doubt worth a few risks to increase circulation in the gutter press."

More long and loud applause.

"I will allow a short response from Mr Green and then call upon professor Marks for his opinion on the accident but for now, your short response, Mr Green."

"All I will add at this stage is. I wonder if Mrs Fordham thinks maybe we should have used the phrase 'is probably dead'? We then might have been accused of vicious unfeeling journalism."

Before the chairman could say anything else, Sharron sharply retorted, "That would be par for the course."

This brought howls of laughter and clapping from the audience.

"It now gives me great pleasure to invite Professor Marks, to talk about the technical investigation into the accident. Professor Marks."

"Before going into the technical details of the investigation, I would like to express my deepest sympathy to Mrs Fordham and Mrs Marsden on their terrible ordeals they have sustained. And I might add, the scurrilous article in the Sunday Clarion must have deeply exacerbated their situations."

Loud cries of 'here, here!' Conrad Green just scowled and remained grim-faced during the rest of the show.

"When my team and I were called to investigate, one thing above all bothered us. How could it have been possible for the off-side wheel of the timber Lorry stay in place all the way from north Scotland and then suddenly fly off the front axle? We know that the vehicle was travelling between fifty and seventy miles per hour up to the time it crashed, as a result of the front wheel coming off. We thoroughly checked both the wheel and axle. Neither showed any signs of wear and tear. The threads of the retaining nuts were in good order as were the nuts which we gathered up. We set up a computerised simulation of the lorry's journey, both with and without the oncoming vehicles at Brooklyn Edge. My team came to the conclusion that on the basis of the scientific evidence and the basic laws of physics, the reason for the wheel coming off remains a mystery.

With regard to the heat generated by the fuel tanker explosion and the burning timber, was such that if any of the passengers could not have left the scene within less than twelve minutes, they could not have survived.

"So, did the three drivers managed to survive?"

"The easy answer to that, Chairman, is that in all three vehicles, the cabins were distorted in such a way the fire service rescue team were able to remove them without too much difficulty."

The Chairman then asked, "One final question, professor. The women who were saved, described the two men who managed to free them from the wrecked bus answered to the photos of the two missing men. Is it possible to calculate how long would it have taken them to free, not only the two women themselves, but also their two young daughters?"

"Although we cannot say with one hundred per cent accuracy, it would seem again, according to computer simulation plus what the rescued ladies told us, it must have taken at least seven or eight minutes to free them from the wreckage, plus the time taken for them to take the four females some seventy or eighty yards from the wreckage. We are looking at ten to eleven minutes from the time they began rescuing the ladies. The factor that must be put into the equation is, how soon after crash did the men begin freeing the ladies? That is crucial for our calculation and we have no way, with any certainty to know what that time interval was."

The presenter then asked, "If, as I understand it, on the basis of twelve minutes, minus eight minutes. That leaves four minutes between the time they recovered from their positions in the wrecked bus until they were able to free the two women and their children, am I correct?"

"That's about right. Of course, if we are out by one or two minutes from either stage, then there is no way either of the men could have survived."

At this point, Sharron intervened, "Mr Chairmen, in view of what the professor has said, my husband and Mrs

Marsden's husband could have had enough time to flee the scene. Had they decided to ignore the cries for help from the two lady passengers, surely then the act of freeing the ladies could not have been the act of two embezzlers. This evidence proves, to any sensible person, that the Sunday Clarion article was utter drivel."

Tremendous applause all round.

"I see we are almost out of time. But, in all fairness, I would like Conrad Green to say a quick few words in defence of his newspaper."

"Despite all the so-called scientific evidence, there is no way anyone can say that there is no truth at all in our article."

At this, professor Marks stood up and leant across the table, visibly angry.

"Excuse me, Mr Green. My opinions are based on scientific facts. You should further know, that I have had more than thirty-five years in engineering, both civil and military in more than ten countries. The team that worked with me on this investigation have between them, more than two hundred years practical experience in engineering. May I ask, what experience and or engineering qualification do you have?"

"I have not any such experience, only a simple logical brain."

"In that case, logically you are not qualified to criticise or question my qualified opinion. If your logic is what you use to edit your so called newspaper, let me remind you—in first year primary school, children are taught how to read and write. And your so-called logic should tell you that engineering science is taught at technical college and higher schools of learning. Therefore, may I respectfully suggest that you go back to primary school and learn how to read and write properly?"

The applause that followed was long and loud.

"That's all we have time for, today. Thank you all for coming and good bye."

In a comfortable, semi-detached house somewhere in north Leeds, Tracey, her husband Sid and three-year-old twin sons Simon and Leonard, whom everyone called Lenny, were watching the Sunday programme about missing persons. Simon was enthralled, after all, he was one of them. It was great seeing Sharron again. She was beautiful as ever and boy, did she give that horrible Conrad Green some stick.

"I wonder what Simon made of all that? There are times I think he knows more than he lets on."

"Nay, lass what could a mere three-year-old make of it?"

Simon had managed to keep silent about who he really was and that he wasn't very impressed with his new parents. Although they were very kind, they were a couple of thickos and somewhat boring. He wasn't sure when to surprise them with his adult mentality. He climbed down off the chair and standing in the middle of the room said, 'That Conrad Green is a diabolical idiot who is not fit to boil an egg, never mind, edit a Sunday Newspaper."

The shock effect on his mother and father was something like expected. Tracey, who had just taken a swig of tea began chocking and dropped the cup and saucer on the carpet. Sid just sat back in his armchair, mouth open, wide.

"Careful, dad, you'll end up catching flies. Maybe someone should fetch a cloth from the kitchen. We can't live with a tea stained carpet."

Simon called over to Lenny.

"Lenny, what's up with mam and dad? They look bewildered."

Lenny could put a simple sentence together, like most three year olds. He just said, "Mam and dad look strange."

"I'll get a cloth, Tracy. Where are they, exactly?"

164

"You'll find one in the cupboard under the kitchen sink."
Tracey's voice was barely audible. When Sid returned, he
turned to the twins and said, "I want to talk to your mother in
private, so go upstairs to your room and find something to do."

"I know what you want to talk about. Let me save you the
trouble of wondering how I am so mature. It's perfectly
simple. I'm, what is known as, an infant prodigy. It's nothing
to be scared of. Oh, dad. Can I have your chess set and board?
I'll teach Lenny the rudiments of the game."

"Okay, Simon."

He went to the sideboard cupboard and passed the board
with box and chessmen to Simon.

"If you like, dad, I'll save you a game later. But I should
warn, you I'm pretty good."

With the twins leaving the room, Sid and Tracey stared
blankly at each other.

Sid was the first to speak.

"Best thing we can do is, to go out for a drink tonight. In
the meantime, let's think about what we'll have for lunch.
Also, it might be a good idea if we both get a notebook and
pencil and if we have an idea, we jot it down."

"Sounds good to me. Shall we just phone for a pizza for
lunch?"

"Yes, sure. That'll be just right. Come to think of it, I saw
Simon looking at a newspaper last week. I wonder if he can
read? Hang on, he was looking at the stocks and shares list in
the financial section. The more I think about it, the more
confusing it gets."

"Come on, Sid. We did say we'll talk about it tonight."

"Yeah, you're right. Bit of a shock though. It'll take some
getting used to. I wonder if he'll teach Lenny a few things."

"They do get on well, together. In fact, even when they
were babies, they never ever fought with each other. Anyway,

what we need now is a good laugh. What's on telly? I could do with watching a Carry-on film."

Sid, scratching his head, and twirling his tongue around his mouth and forcing a smile at Tracey. She recognised the signs. He wanted something that he thought she might not approve of. She decided that whatever it is, she would go along with it.

"Why do I get the idea that you want to do something? What is it?"

"The truth is, I'm feeling restless and…"

Before he could finish what he wanted to say, Tracey interjected, "You want to go for a stroll in the sunshine. I'm right aren't I?"

"I don't know how you can read my mind, but as always you are spot on."

"It's what is known as wife-ology or how to read your husband's mind without really trying. Anyway, don't waste time talking put on a warm coat and get going. Just don't be late for lunch. We'll eat at about one."

Sid got out of his chair, walked over to Tracey and kissed her cheek.

"I certainly picked a winner when I chose you. You are an absolute gem."

"Go on, away with you before I throw up. Any idea what you want for lunch?"

"How about egg, chips, and beans?"

"I don't suppose a few fried sausages as well would be okay too."

"Know what, Tracey, I don't deserve you."

Tracey smiled and pretending to be annoyed, said, "Will you get on your way already, move."

Sid was tempted to pay a further compliment but decided against it.

He just said, "Right, I am off. See you at one."

A little while later, Tracey realised that they would need a baby-sitter for this evening. The girl who usually did it, may have arranged something for this evening. Better phone Ann now and see if she's free.

"Hello, Tracey Smith calling. Is Ann available?"

Tracey could hear the voice at the other end shouting, "Ann it's for you, Mrs Smith."

After a few seconds, Ann took the receiver, "Hello, Mrs Smith."

"Hope you are okay, Ann, and not too busy. I hope I haven't interrupted anything."

"No, not really. I am just doing some revision for the GCSE exams."

"I know it's short notice, but, by any chance, could you baby sit for us this evening? Something has cropped up and we have to go out. I'll pay you double the usual rate because it is the weekend and as I say, it is short notice. I don't like bothering you over a weekend because I know it's probably the only time you have for leisure. Is there any chance you could come over? The twins have improved their behaviour since you were last here. I'm sure they'll be no bother."

"Okay, Mrs Smith. I'll be there. What time do you want me at your place?"

"If we say we'll call for you at seven and will give you lift back. You are a real treasure, Ann. As usual, we'll leave some sandwiches and of course you can make yourself a hot drink whenever you want. So, we'll see you at seven. Bye for now."

"Bye, Mrs Smith"

Ann was not all that happy about the situation. The double money was the attraction. But the twins! They could be a pest at times. Lenny wasn't too bad, but that Simon was such a cheeky, devil always touching her legs and wanting to kiss and cuddle her. She thought strange that one so young could be so affectionate. Still, 'money is money, as it all helps.'

So, just before seven, a toot on the Smith's car and grabbing her note books and pen, Ann was on her way to the Smith's home.

"Now, you two. It's upstairs to bed. You can listen to the radio for a while. I want you to be really good boys. We don't want to upset Ann because she won't come here again."

Taking the twins to their bedroom and making sure they were properly in their night clothes, Tracey told the twins that she asked Ann to come up and switch the radio off in half an hour.

"No need to bother Ann. I can tell the time mam."

The confident manner of Simon took Tracey aback, slightly.

"You are full of surprises today, Simon. Good night, you two. Be good."

As soon as Simon heard the sound of the car pulling away, he sneaked out of the bedroom and quietly went downstairs. Ann was sitting at the dinner table.

"Hello, Ann. Nice to see you. What are you reading?"

"My! My! You have come on since I last saw you. Shouldn't you be in bed?"

"I'm not sleepy. Let me see what you are reading."

"You won't understand it. Besides, it's boring. I don't think Economics is for young children."

"I don't agree. Does your book say anything about the Malthusian trap or does just go into the ideas of J. M. Keynes?"

The reaction of Ann could only be described as a cross between shock and incredulity.

"Where, when, and how did you learn of such things? You are only just three years old and couldn't possibly know of such things."

"Ann, please calm down. I'm, what they call in the classics, as an infant prodigy. So, let me sit on your knee I'll look at your note book and advise you what to write down."

"Okay, but no touching or kissing. I must finish my homework and revision."

"Okay, it's a deal."

Ann lifted him up and Simon looked at her work books. He shook his head disapprovingly.

"Just make a note of these book titles I'll give you, or at least write down a few quotes such as, 'In the USA, a law was passed called the 'Smoot-Hawley Act'. It was to do with protectionism. In some countries, it was called Customs Duty or Tariffs'. By the way Tariff is an Arabic word."

"Your mother never said anything about your abilities." By the tone of her voice, Simon felt she was still in a state of abject surprise. The one she must not do, is blab to all and sundry about him.

"Ann, please promise me you'll not mention anything about me to anyone. I don't want to give interviews or sign autographs. Oh! And by the way, my mam and dad only found out this morning about my abilities. So please, not a word to anyone."

"What I don't understand is, why you and not Lenny? Or maybe Lenny too is also advanced for his age."

"Lenny is quite bright. Today, I taught him the rudiments of Chess and so far, he is good for the first three moves. I'm sure he will improve with practice."

Still feeling somewhat bemused by Simon, she suddenly blurted out, "Besides Economics, what else do you know?"

"I like Math, but my favourite interests are Cricket and Tennis."

"Is there anything else you know that might be helpful to me in Economics?"

"Let me see. Find and read any book by or about Adam Smith, also read about the history of Taxation. Do you like History as a subject?"

"Some of it. Why do you ask?"

"Because, if you write about Economics in an historical perspective, that will impress the examiners. Do you think you might like to work in a bank or accountants when you leave school?"

"I was hoping to get a place in university, eventually."

"A complete waste of time. All you'll learn is how to drink and have sex. Besides, you'll have to start your working life with a whacking great debt hanging over your head. It's not worth it. Anyway, what subject were you wanting to study?"

"I would like to take English."

"No good. If you were interested in Math and science, then perhaps it might be worthwhile."

"Well, you've certainly given me a lot to think about. Don't you think it's about time you were back in?"

"I'll go if you give me a nice kiss."

Ann obliged and smiling, said, "There you are! Now, off you go."

As Simon was leaving, he turned to face Ann.

"Don't say too much to mam and dad about what our conversations. I have a funny feeling they would want to make it public so they could charge for interviews and the like. You do understand?"

"Okay, promise."

The sound of the Smiths car pulling-up, made Ann start. Was it that time already. Looking at the clock, she smiled. Time had moved on so very quickly. The question was, should she mention anything about her conversation with Simon. She was feeling tired and was looking forward to a good night's sleep.

"Are you ready to be off, then?" asked Mr Smith.

"Yes, have got all my books and I'm looking forward to my bed."

Tracey, trying to sound nonchalant, asked, "Did the twins give you any trouble?"

"Not at all. How was your evening?"

"Nice, thank you for asking and here is your reward."

"Thanks, very much. I'm always willing to come here. So if you are planning a night out, you know my phone number."

"Thank you, Ann. My regards to your parents."

Not so long after, Sid came back after dropping Ann off at her home.

"Sid, did you have the impression that Ann was a little too quick in wanting to get back home?"

"No, not at all. As she said, she was very tired or words to that effect. Why do you think she was too quick to leave? What possible other reason could she have had?"

"This is the first time she has ever asked about how we enjoyed our outing."

"I think you are making a two plus two equals five. Like all youngsters, as they grow up, become aware of the usual social graces."

The following morning was holiday for Tracey. Ever since flex time was introduced in the council offices where she worked, as a general assistant to in the Chief Maintenance Manger, the extra odd days made life much more comfortable after Friday night and the weekend. Today, however, the situation regarding Simon and indeed Lenny called for careful planning. Next week, she had intended to start them off at a private nursery school. Heaven knows, how the teachers would cope with him, and what about the other children. How would they react?"

Sid could take off time whenever he wanted. The fact that he worked for himself made it almost impossible to have time off at all. As a watchmaker, jeweller and a dealer in antiques,

171

he was either at his workshop or working a market stall. Today, however, he had arranged for a wealthy collector to view a long case clock that he had renovated and was standing in the hall. It had a loud tick and was getting in Tracey's way. Still, she did not complain because it would sell around a thousand pounds and that was not, as her mother used to say, to be sneezed at.

Sid came down the stairs, looking dapper in his light brown suit, white shirt and bow tie to match.

"Well, look who's here. Mr 'All dolled up' and ready for action. Wonderful, I am impressed."

"I feel inspired by your vote of confidence. The client should be here in about ten. In the meantime, what's for breakfast?"

"You don't want to smell of anything strong. So, its yoghurt, orange juice followed by a slice of toast and coffee. How does that sound? By the way, where are the twins?"

"Lenny is upstairs playing with one of his toys and Simon is in the back room, looking at yesterday's newspapers. Did I say Simon? Maybe I should have said young Einstein." Tracey couldn't help grinning.

"Now, remember what we said last night in the pub. We treat him just as any parent deals with any three-year-old. We know he thinks like an adult and talks like one. We don't know if he was born with the power to read or write. What's more, maybe he knows one or two foreign languages as well."

"After breakfast, we can casually ask him if there is anything interesting in the papers."

"Good idea. I think his abilities he must have inherited from your family genes. My lot were not all that bright."

"Don't say that, Sid. Look how bright you are."

"Me? Bright! What do you mean?"

"Well, you married me."

Sid burst into laughter.

"I certainly walked right into that one. Mind you, I must agree there could be something in what you say."

"Sit down and I'll make your breakfast."

Perhaps, it was half an hour later, maybe a bit longer, but when Sid and Tracey looked back at what happened that Monday morning, they could not be sure of anything. As they were about to speak to Simon, the phone rang. It was the potential buyer of the long case clock. He was in the area now so would it be convenient form to call in a few minutes.

"Certainly, we've had breakfast, so you can come as soon as you like." Sid deliberately kept his voice clear but expressionless. He did not want to give the impression that he would be so glad to sell at any price.

Soon the door chimes announced the arrival of the customer.

"Come in, sir. Can we offer you a coffee or tea?"

"No, thanks, Mr Smith. Had breakfast not long ago so I'm okay. I take it, this is the clock in question."

"Yes, if I switch the hall light on, you'll get a better picture of the wood grain. My wife says things look different in electric light than they do in natural light. I can't say that I've noticed the difference all that much. But it's always best to agree with one's wife."

The client laughed.

"I suppose you are like me, always in the wrong."

"I hate to admit it, but she usually is right. So, what do you think? It certainly does have a different appearance with light on."

"True and I do like it. So, if we can agree on a price, I'll take it."

"As I said in our first conversation, I am looking at around One Thousand Five hundred pounds but I'm open to any sensible offer."

"How does Eleven Five hundred sound? And will you accept a cheque?"

"Certainly."

"And, what if, I were to offer a straight thousand cash here and now?"

Sid paused, then said, "We have a deal."

The buyer pulled out his bulging wallet and counted out one thousand pounds in fifty pound notes.

"Right, I'll give you a hand to load it into your van."

"My lad's in the car. He's a big, hefty lad and the exercise will do him good."

It was then, that Sid went into the back room. Simon was looking sad. There were tears in his eyes.

"What on earth's the matter, Simon? Does something hurt you?"

"No."

"Where is your mother? Has she been in to talk to you or anything?"

"'No, she has taken Lenny out for a walk in the park. She said he was feeling restless."

"Didn't you want to go with them?"

"No. I've been reading in yesterday's paper, article about a three-year-old in Baltimore. He is a born musician. Born the same day as me."

"So, why is that making you sad?"

"It's not that, exactly, dad. You see, I know why he keeps having those awful nightmares."

"I haven't read the article, Simon. I'll just have a gander now. Then we can talk about it. Okay?"

"It's not just about him, dad, there is something else. I hoped that somehow I could keep the truth from you and mam, but it seems I'll have to tell you and you won't believe me and you won't love me anymore. I just couldn't bear that. You're so good to me and Lenny."

Sid was totally confused.

"Tell you what, Simon. Just let me read this article then you can tell me what is bothering you and I promise, mother and I will always love you no matter what the problem is. That's what mothers and fathers are for."

Sid picked up the paper and began to read. It was the first time he had known about Leroy Washington. He wondered if Tracey had heard of him. His mother, the soprano, Maria Washington, was world famous and Sid did recall something about giving birth just after a concert in her hometown of Baltimore. While Sid was reading, Simon was pacing up and down and his crying was becoming intense.

"Come here, Simon. Sit on my knee and we will have a man to man talk. Afterwards, we will talk to mother when she gets back. Maybe, we will have lunch first. Now, come on, tell me nice and easy just what the matter is."

"Okay, but promise you won't be upset or angry at what I'm going to tell you."

"I promise, Simon. But first, let me put the answer phone on."

Simon climbed down off his father's knee. Sid went over to the phone.

"Do you want to tell now what's bothering you, Simon? Are you okay sitting on the floor or do you want to sit on my knee?"

"I'll stay here dad, thank you."

"Okay, Simon I'm all ears. Maybe, you should begin by saying why you know Leroy Washington is having nightmares?"

"The reason is, dad, he was warned by the angel in charge to stay calm if he had flashbacks about the accident and our experience at the reception centre of the next world." Simon paused and looked for some expression in his father's face.

175

"There are two questions, I must ask. The first one is, you mentioned the angel in charge. You also said our experience: not his experience. Can you explain?"

"I can, dad and this what I have been dreading about telling you. Anyway, here goes. I said our experience because I was there as well."

Despite a great effort, Simon burst in to a flood of tears and ran towards Sid who lifted him up and kissed him.

"Nice and easy Simon, slowly, now calm yourself. Dad is here and I'm listening. You carry on in your own time nice and easy."

"Dad, you are a wonderful man."

Sid laughed gently. "That's what I try and tell your mother but she doesn't always agree with me."

It was Simon's turn to laugh.

"That's what wives are for. To keep us men in our place."

Sid looked really puzzled. On one hand, Simon was behaving like a mature adult male, but emotionally he was just like any other three-year-old.

"Go on. You said you and Leroy Washington were at the reception centre of the next world. So, how did you come to be there?"

"You'll find this so hard to understand, dad, but believe me, it is one hundred per cent true. Do you remember, about three years ago, the crash at Brooklyn Edge?"

"Of course, I do. We were watching that programme yesterday all about it."

"Well, you know how that professor couldn't work out why they could not find the remains of the two men, Martin Marsden and Jeff Fordham."

"Go on, Simon. Take it easy; nice and slow."

"Well, the reason is, that after they rescued the two women and their daughters, their bodies as well as their souls were taken by mistake to the next world reception centre." Simon paused and looked tearfully into his father's eyes.

Sid, who at best, could be described as an agnostic, could only stare blankly at Simon.

"Simon, would you mind if I just walked around the back garden whilst I mull over what you have just told me? Will you be all right on your own for just a little while?"

"Okay, dad. I know it's hard for you to take it in but there is more to tell."

Sid, at first, walked around the garden looking at each plant and shrub trying to put together all that Simon had told him. He then sat in a garden chair, his head placed in his cupped hands, elbows resting on his knees. Could it be that Simon had been having vivid dreams? But how would that explain his ability to read. There was definitely something very strange going on. He thought it best to hear what else Simon had to say. He strolled back in to the house.

"You might as well tell me everything, Simon. You mentioned the two missing men from the accident were taken to the Reception centre of the next world by mistake. Who actually made the mistake?"

"It was the angelic clerks."

"So, what happened to the two men and their bodies?"

"Because of the mistake, the only way for Martin Marsden and Jeff Fordham could be returned to this world was to put them in new bodies. In other words, we were reborn."

"Now, hang on a second. You said we were reborn. So who are you Simon? Are you really my son or what?"

"That's what I have been dreading to tell you. Martin Marsden is now called Leroy Washington and I am Jeff Fordham. So, now you know and I'm so upset for you, mam, Lenny and my old friend Martin Marsden."

"Don't say anything to your mother, just yet."

"Does anyone else know what you've told me?"

"Last night I helped Ann with her homework and revision. I asked her not to say anything. The only reason I'm telling you now is because of what's happening to my old friend, Martin Marsden, who is now Leroy Washington. It was when I read about his nightmares in the paper, it upset me because he was warned that he'd been given the musical abilities he would experience these recurring dreams and flashbacks of the accident."

"So, what about you?"

"I said I just wanted to be myself and did not want any special abilities, by way of compensation. To tell the truth, dad, I thought I was in a hospital and that it was all dream. If you remember, when I was born, I had a shaking fit. That was because I realised it was not a dream. Oh there is something else. You see the three spot birthmark? This happened when I asked Martin to pinch me. I did the same to him."

"Simon, or should I call you Jeff?"

"Please, you know me as Simon and that is who I will be."

"I'm still not sure I can take this all in. I have no idea what your mam will say. I need to think."

"I understand, dad. If there is anything you might think of that could prove what I've said, just say the word."

"For the time being, I can't think of anything specific. You see, I'm not sure there is such a thing as the next world. Maybe there is, maybe not. But the fact that you are a child prodigy makes me wonder."

"The truth is, dad, I'm not a child prodigy. I'm a thirty-one-year-old Accountant in the body of a three-year-old child. And Martin Marsden is the same age as mine, in the body of Leroy Washington who is also three years old. We were born on the same day."

"Anyway, I am feeling hungry. Mam will soon be home so we'll have lunch together."

"Don't suppose you fancy a game of chess till mam and Lenny get back?"

"Sure, why not?"

Chapter Twelve
A Birth and a New Job

Two days after the original date of the sensational Sunday programme that witnessed the contretemps between Professor Marks and Conrad Green, Louise went into labour and presented the world with a boy, who everyone said, was the image of his father. Louise, surrounded by her sisters and well-wishers, could only think about how she could find time to work, pay the bills and who would look after the baby. She hadn't time even to think of a name. Mildred and Helen took turns to visit her for the first two weeks after the birth. No one could think of any solution to her financial difficulties. The Government allowance was hardly a fortune. Although, Helen and her Husband gave her a non-repayable loan for the baby to start life with. Louise realised life from now on was going to be a struggle. Perhaps, a qualified nanny would be a great help. But, they too, needed payment.

By a stroke of luck, a new neighbour with a new baby moved in just across the road. The husband was civilian technical specialist at an army depot and Selma was a jewellery designer who worked from home. They could afford a nanny, so when Louise approached them and asked if she brings her baby across and makes a contribution to the fees, they were delighted to help.

As the weeks went by, Louise wanted to do some work. The supermarket was cutting back to save on expenses, so there was no opening there.

One evening, Mildred phoned and asked if she fancied a job in a small office.

"What sort of firm are we talking about?"

"It's my gentleman's friend's cousin, who runs a small building firm. Kitchens, Bricklaying and that sort of thing. The lady who worked there has decided to emigrate and is leaving in a week. It just a bit of typing, invoicing telephone work. I'm sure you could do it quite easily."

"Where is his place?"

"Not that far from you. On the way to Leeds. If you like, I can fetch him around sometime tomorrow evening. Will that be okay?"

"Yes sure. What time?"

"About Seven thirty. Is that okay?"

"Sure, till tomorrow then. Bye and thanks very much, Mildred."

As usual, Mildred who thrived on punctuality and the man arrived as the clock chimed the half hour. Louise, trying hard not show how impressed by the rugged muscular appearance of Mildred's companion, almost forgot that her mouth was wide open. Turning to face the gentleman, Mildred said, "It seems Clive, my sister Louise has already taken a shine to you."

"Mildred, please. What will?" looking quizzically at Mildred.

"Clive, Clive Hanbury."

"She always likes to embarrass me, Clive. She has been that way since we were kids."

"I'm a little confused, you called your sister, Mildred, I know her as June."

"There's a lot of family history to it, Clive. Eventually, our parents agreed the names should be June Mildred. Father insisted that, between ourselves, it would be Mildred in the home and June in the outside world."

Soon, the three of them were enjoying tea and chocolate biscuits.

"Why don't I go upstairs and see how my baby nephew is going on whilst you two, if you'll pardon the expression, get down to business."

"What did I tell you, Clive, any opportunity to embarrass me?"

Smiling, Clive opened the zip of his document case and passed two A4 sheets to her.

"The top sheet is all about me and the firm and the second is a job description. I suggest you have a read then ask me any questions."

As he passed her the papers, their fingers touched. Louise felt a peculiar sensation, that much to her regret, she enjoyed. On one hand, she felt deeply excited about Clive's appearance and sexy tone of voice, on the other hand, she longed for Martin. Passion and guilt not being the most stable of cocktails, Louise became angry and confused. Another unstable cocktail mixture. So much so, her eyes, all of a blur, she did not realise that holding the sheets upside were causing an irritation.

Pretending not to notice, Clive, ever the diplomat, asked, "Have I given you the right papers? I do have a lot of items in my wallet and I may have passed you the wrong ones."

Louise lost no time in straightening the papers.

"No, it's okay. I had them wrong way round."

By now, she gradually returned to normal and deliberately reading slowly, felt that the job sounded quite interesting. The working conditions, in particular—hours to suit were appealing.

Clearing her throat, but not quite managing to conceal nervousness, she said, "I'm sure I could soon adapt to your clerical system. I take it, you are computerised?"

"Yes, however I do have an old fashion typewriter just in case of a computer breakdown. Also, there is a manual back up system for the same reason. As a one-man business, I can't afford any delays to clients or suppliers."

Louise felt hesitant about what she was about to ask. It was though something that could not be avoided.

"I need to know two things before we talk about wages. The first is, you know I have an infant and sometimes they have these childhood illnesses that can come on unexpectedly, which would mean I wouldn't be able to come in—would that be a big problem?"

"My old uncle, Dave, who is something of a store man and does odd jobs around the yard, would step in for a while, so in answer to your question, it would not be a big problem because I would be paying you by the hour, you would not lose money."

"That seems fair enough."

"And your second question is?"

"What do I call you?"

"Everyone calls me Clive, except when there are customers and strangers in the office."

There followed a brief moment of subdued embarrassment. A case of who should speak next and what to say.

Louise then stepped in, "We have not discussed wages yet. So, what figure did you have in mind?"

Clive reached into his breast pocket, pulled out a small notebook and wrote a figure then passed it to Louise.

"You'd be on a six-month trial. If all goes well, there will be a twenty-five percent increase."

Louise looked at the figure. It was lower than she hoped for but with twenty-five per cent increase, it would be acceptable. The truth is, that she had no option but to accept. "When can I start?"

"Tomorrow. I'll pick you up at a quarter to eight. Is that okay?"

"Yes, that'll be fine."

"Well, I promised June I'd give her a lift home, so if she's finished playing with your son, we'll be off."

On their way out, Louise called Mildred back. With eyes full of tears, she chokingly said, "I don't know if I can ever thank you enough. I'm just up to here with gratitude."

"Get on with, you daft thing. If I can't help my sister, then who should I help? In any case, it's Clive who has given you the chance for a new life."

Embracing, the two sisters kissed and Mildred joined Clive in the car.

Chapter Thirteen
Sharron is Angry and Confused

"Hello, Sharron Fordham."

"Good evening, Mrs Fordham, Detective Inspector James speaking. Sorry calling so late. We were unable to contact you this morning. We've been in touch with Willows and Sanford regarding the investigation into the Landon Margo account. They told us that your husband would take work home and we need to view any documents that might be in your apartment."

Sharron, who was always on a short fuse, angrily replied, "Inspector!! I'm sure you are aware that my husband is listed as a missing person and therefore all his accounts are frozen and the court controls them."

"I am aware of the situation, Mrs Fordham and we are in touch with the court."

"Well, until I hear from the court that they have given permission, you may not come here. Do I make myself clear?"

"I appreciate what you are saying, but you do realise that this a criminal investigation and as such there is a legal obligation to co-operate with the police."

"I hope, inspector that you are not implying that my husband is, in any way, involved in the embezzlement."

By now, Sharron's temperament was reaching the point of lost control.

"In that case, go to the court. Thank you and Good night!" Sharron slamming down the receiver, then making her way to the drinks cabinet, vowed to contact the press, both local and national. She wasn't sure if newspapers had editorial staff on duty at all hours. Deciding to take a chance, she dialled the Morning Post. The line was engaged.

So, taking a swig of Gin, she re-dialled. Luck was on her side. A few moments later, a calm voice slowly intoned, "News desk, please state your name and press hash key." Feeling irritated, Sharron listened to the options 'For foreign news press one, for local news press two, for all other items press three.' Pressing three and letting out an angry breath of frustration, Sharron felt her hackles rising.

"News Desk, Crane Bradley. Hello Sharron how can I help?"

"I want to report a case of harassment by the police."

"In what way?"

"They insist doing a search of my home. They say it has to do with the Landon Margo embezzlement affair."

"Just wait a few moments while I check our files."

True to his word, after a short while, he said, "I see your husband was the accountant in charge of the account and that he is now listed as a missing person. So, I take it, that they have permission via the court to…"

"No, they have not been to the court. That is my complaint. They are deliberately side stepping the court because they want to make him the thief. It is not fair! Can you help me?"

"I'll tell you what we'll do. We'll contact the police and see what they have to say. Do you have a police name we can refer to?"

"Yes, it was Detective Inspector James."

"Right, leave it with me and I'll get back to you asap."

"Thank you, very much. I look forward to hearing from you."

About an hour or so later, Crane Bradley, true to his word, phoned Sharron, with the news that after contacting the courts and the police, a compromise had been reached. Because the police did not want a bad press, they would only search Sharron's flat when it would be convenient with a Morning Post representative also present to see fair play.

So, in the following Sunday's edition of the Morning Post, the arrangement and the Paper's involvement were given front page billing.

At breakfast, in the Smith household, Sid, lounging in his favourite armchair, munching toast and marmalade read out loud, "I see the police are going to search Sharron Fordham's flat."

Simon, who was playing chess with Lenny turned to face Sid. Waving his hand, attracting Sid's attention and calling out in a loud whisper, "Dad, need to talk with you private."

Sid, momentarily looking startled, said, "Simon, there's something in the back garden I must show you."

"Can I come too?" Lenny asked.

He was not in a good position chess wise and any excuse not to continue would be a welcome relief. Sid came to Simon's rescue.

"No, Lenny, I need to have a word with Simon about his behaviour at the nursery school. He'll be back soon."

With that, he and Simon headed for the back garden. "Okay, Simon, what's on your mind?"

"Dad, we mustn't let the police search the Fordham's home till the contents of the home safe are removed."

"I don't understand. How do you know about what's..." His voice trailing off to a puzzled silence. It dawned on him that if Simon is, or was Jeff Fordham, then of course he would know what is in her flat. Sid was still having problems coming to terms with the fact that three-year-old Simon was Sharron Fordham's Husband.

"What's in the safe? In any case, why can't she open the safe and remove the contents?"

187

"She does not have the combination. It is my private safe. And if the police get hold of it, they will open it even if they use brute force which means they'll see the expensive jewellery that I've bought over the years. They'll think that Sharron and I were involved in the Landon Margo affair."

"So, what we need to do is let her know the combination. I suppose we could phone her and…"

"No good, dad. I'll bet the police are tapping her phone. Besides, even if we spoke to her on her mobile, she'll think it's a crank call."

"So, any ideas as to how we should contact her?"

"I was thinking we should go over to her office. I know where she works."

"I see, so all we need do is, let her know the combination."

"Not quite that simple, dad. You see, there is an ordinary latch key type lock that opens up to another door where the combination lock is situated. The problem is, I could never remember the combinations numbers off by heart. I wrote it down, and the note paper as well as the latch key are kept on my side of the dressing table drawers."

"Why on earth didn't you tell her the combination?!!"

"I only wanted the diamonds, instead of a life insurance policy. I put the combination details in my will that I deposited with my solicitor."

Sid frowned. This situation was something of a shock. What possible excuse could he invent for visiting Mrs Fordham at her place of work? As if Simon was reading his mind, he said, "We could say we have an urgent message from someone who knew Jeff."

"She might think it could be a trick by a reporter trying to get an interview."

"Good point dad, I know. Let's write a note, giving her all the gen. We could hand it over to the receptionist. Tell you what, you write it now. I'll tell you what to put."

Soon, they were on the way to Sharron's workplace. They were lucky. There was nobody waiting at reception. Sid bounded over, looked around to see if anyone was within hearing distance. There were a few people sitting in plush chairs looking at magazines. Nevertheless, Sid thought it best to whisper as loudly as possible.

"I need to get a message to Mrs Fordham. I need to do it now. It is very urgent."

The receptionist looked puzzled.

"I'll phone her office, sir and see if she is available."

In what seemed like an age, the response was, "Mrs Fordham is very busy and cannot be disturbed."

Sid looked and felt agitated.

"Please, phone her again and say an old friend of her husband has some information that she must act upon. If she won't see me then, can you or somebody giver her this envelope. I repeat it must be done now."

"I'm sorry sir, I cannot leave my counter and there is no one else at the moment who is available." Simon tugged at Sid's jacket.

"I know where her office is, dad, I'll take it up to her." With that, he took Sid's hand and they walked towards a flight of stairs. They reached the first floor and noticed at the far end was a lady stepping out of the female toilets.

"Dad, it's her!"

Sid, taken aback for a moment, just stood still not knowing what to do next. All the while, the lady, walking towards them, suddenly stopped outside an office door and was about to enter.

"Dad, call out before she goes in!"

Sid, gulping, shouted out, "Mrs Fordham, I have a letter for you—urgent."

By this time, Sid and Simon had reached her. Sharron, looking askance, slowly took the envelope and gasped. On the back of it was written, 'To Luscious legs' from Mr Magnificent.'

Sid said, "Look, Mrs Fordham, this letter was given to me by a complete stranger. All he said was, that you need to act upon the instructions before the police searches your flat. That's all I know. "

Simon tugged at his dad's sleeve. "Tell her it's about how to open my safe."

"Thanks for reminding me, Simon."

Turning to face Sharron, "He did say something about how to open your husband's safe. Can't stop. Must take this young man to his nursery. Come on, Simon lets go. Bye Mrs Fordham."

Chapter Fourteen

Sharron gasped. Shouting at the fleeing figures of Sid and Simon. But to no avail. Stepping into her office, she contacted the main switchboard.

"Have got to go home. Something urgent has cropped up. If anyone asks, tell them I'll be back tomorrow as per usual." So, grabbing her briefcase, she made for the lift. Before leaving the reception area, she noticed that a man who was there before she arrived was sitting in the same chair. He put down his newspaper and got up, following her out. Sharron thought he must be a plain clothes policeman. As if to test her theory, she walked up to her car, stopped, looked around standing still then resting her briefcase on the car bonnet. She opened it, unzipped a section and moved papers giving the impression she was searching for something. All the time, inclining her head this way and that, yes she was right. The man had followed her and was entering his car.

"Okay Boyo. You've met your match with me." She thought.

So, snapping her briefcase shut, she dashed out of the car park and headed towards the office. Sighting a bus that was drawing up to the bus stop, she joined the short queue. She had no idea if the man had followed her. Looking out of the window, she could not see him. As the bus pulled away, she heaved a sigh and opened the envelope. She drew out the paper and read 'Sharron go to my chest of draws. Take out my special, purple pajama jacket—the one you like. Inside the

191

pocket, there is a key and a note with numbers written on it. The key will open the outer door to the safe. There is another door with a combination lock. It will open, if you follow the order of the numbers on the note. Love you."

For once, in her life, Sharron was utterly confused. On one hand, she felt the note was genuine. But who was the man who handed it to her? What connection did he have with Jeff? Was Jeff still alive? If so, where was he? Also, why would he be hiding? It was not all that long, when the bus stopped near her flat. The car that was usually parked opposite was not there. This meant that the car parked in the office's car park was the police car. Wasting no time, she dashed into the building and into her flat hurrying to the chest of drawers, took out Jeff's pyjama jacket and with trembling hands, withdrew the envelope from the pocket. As written in the note, there it was: the key. Also, the paper with eight numbers written on it. The excitement increased as her heart pounded, beads of perspiration appeared on her brow. She hesitated. With a gulp she left the bedroom. Key and note still in her hand, she opened the drinks cabinet and grabbed the gin bottle. Decided not to open it. Shouting out, 'Sharron Fordham. Pull yourself together, silly, stupid bitch. This is not you. Calm down and open the bloody safe.' Sharron did not like being out of control. She did not like the anger which compounded the feeling. By the time she returned to the bedroom, and opened the safe, she was at fever pitch. After opening the safe drawers and seeing the contents, shock and delight altered her mood. In the shelf trays, were diamond bracelets, necklaces, trays of rings: Golden and diamonds. That was just the top two trays. But what startled her the most was, the handwritten note which read. 'Sharron, if you are reading this, it means I'm no longer in this world. Perhaps, even dead.' Sharron could not suppress a wary smile. Jeff's insatiable sense of humour had once more burst forth. 'As you know, I'd didn't believe in life insurance policies. Instead, all that you see is worth at least a quarter of a million. So, be happy and think of me sometimes. Jeff.'

Now, What?!! Only Jeff had that info. So, who was that man with the child? How did he get hold of the info? Only Jeff could have given it to him. So, Jeff must still be alive. So, why did he not get in touch with her? The more she pondered, the more confusion. Back to the gin bottle. She poured out a treble. Maybe a cigarette would slow down her racing mind. She settled for the gin. Then her mobile sent out its incoming call fanfare. It was the Daily Post

"The police are getting impatient. How soon can they come?"

"I've a lot on, at the office. Tomorrow evening, say any time after seven. Is that okay with you?"

"We'll check with police and call back to confirm." Sharron agreed. So, now what. First things first. Remove and hide contents of the safe. Then, what! Maybe she should put in the safe a few surprises for police. There were lots of copies of Jeff's accountancy magazines. With first a black marker pen, she wrote on the front covers 'Code A1' then a random line of numbers in red marker. Each magazine, different numbers. After removing all the contents and bagging them up in pillow cases, she closed and locked the safe, tore up the note with the combination and put the key in one of her costume jackets. So, what next? Feeling hungry but no inclination to start cooking or even making up a sandwich, she decided to make her way to the local bakery coffee shop. Looking out the window, she saw the police car.

As she made her way out, an idea struck her. She had not been in touch with Louise for some time. Time to visit her. Some of the jewellery from the safe could help her financially. She was about to cross the road, when a car drew up behind the police car. Out stepped Hal, a close colleague. "Hal! Hang on!" She shouted and dashed across the road. "I'm going to the coffee shop, what are you doing in this neck of the woods?"

"Visiting a client. May I join you first? I'm famished."

"I was just about to ask you."

As they were making their way, Sharron asked, "Will you do me a great favour? The car in front of yours has a plain-clothes policeman inside. He's been watching my block of flats for days."

"So, how can I help?"

"I'd like you to draw up close up to him, while I get Jeff's car and block him in, from the front. I'll, then call a taxi. In that way, he won't be able to follow me."

"So, where are you going that's so secret?"

"Sorry, can't explain now."

Hurrying to the rear of block, she called out, "Will tell you at the office tomorrow."

A bewildered Hal, slowly walked back to his car. He did as Sharron had asked and looked nervously at the car in front. In what seemed an age, but was just a few minutes, a Jaguar parked close in front of the police car. Sharron remained inside and phoned for a taxi. She left the Jag and carrying two shopping bags, ran to Hal. Signalling him to come out, she waved a shopping bag so that the policeman would see. Poor Hal, a somewhat timid soul, could only gasp as she thrust the bag into his hand.

It was not long, before the taxi arrived. Soon, Sharron left it as it stopped outside the address, which was two streets away from Louise's home. That way, if the police decided to interrogate the driver, he could truthfully give them the wrong address.

"What a surprise. Come in, how are you doing?" Louisa, doing her best to sound as though she was interested.

"I took a chance, hoping you'd be in. I have something for you that should help with your finances."

Louisa took the shopping bag. She was puzzled by the tins of beans and other vegetables. Slowly removing them, she saw tissue-covered items, which, after undoing, left her wide-eyed and gasping. Holding three diamond necklaces and several diamond rings and some pearl earrings, she was at a loss as to what to say. Seeing how bewildered Louisa was, Sharron blurted out, "Sorry, can't stop to explain. I'll be in touch. If by any chance, the police should ask about my visit, just say I'd been doing some shopping for you."

With that, she made her way to the front door and left. Louise, confused by what had happened, just stared at the jewellery. Heaven alone knows how much it was all worth.

Where could she sell it all? Perhaps Clive could advise her or, better still, if he would sell it for her, there would be no connection to her or Sharron. It was very confusing. In the meantime, where to put the stuff. And, why did Sharron say the police might visit her? As if, on cue, the front door bell rang. Louise grabbed the jewellery, hurried upstairs to the bedroom and wrapped it in a towel which she put in the linen laundry basket at the bottom of the pile. Making a point of moving very slowly downstairs, she paused briefly by the front door, before opening it. A tall man holding an identity card in front of his face said, "Police, may I come in?"

"I'm rather busy. What do you want?"

"We know that Mrs Fordham has been here. We need to know what was in the shopping bag she was carrying."

"It was a few cans of beans and some lettuce. As I said, I'm busy, so if that's all?"

Louise's voiced trailed off as she moved the door to close it. It was the turn of the policeman to look bewildered. With a sigh and expression that revealed irritation, he said, "Very well, Okay." And left. Without a search warrant, he was powerless.

Back at her flat, Sharron phoned the Daily Post.

"If you and the police are able, you and they can come now."

As expected, the policeman asked Sharron to open the safe.

"Sorry, can't help you. It is my husband's and I have no idea where he keeps the key."

"In that case, we will have to search for it. We'll start in the bedroom." So, the two policemen and the press photographer followed Sharron. They went straight for the chest of drawers and opened Sharron's side.

"If you don't mind, I cannot allow you to go through my things. I've just told you the safe was my husband's private place where he kept all his highly confidential documents. So, it is utterly pointless to go through my things."

"Makes sense to me," said the pressman, taking a picture of the policeman holding the draw handle. The policeman let go of the handle. Grim faced, he turned to face the newsman.

"This is part of an ongoing situation. It is important that the investigation be allowed to proceed without interference."

His voice rasped out the words in a deliberate slow fashion with a menacing slight tone.

"I will have to take the safe to the station where we will open it."

"Excuse me, Sargent, or whatever your rank is, I should not have to remind you that the safe is the personal property of my husband, who is a missing person and as such, all his possessions come under the jurisdiction of the Court."

It was Sharon's turn to glare at the policeman. She continued, "So, without the court's consent, I cannot allow you to remove the safe."

"I believe the lady does have a point," the pressman smiled as he spoke. He was enjoying the policeman's discomfort. There followed an uncomfortable silence.

Taking his mobile from his front pocket, the police officer spoke to the person in charge at the station. A few moments later, he said, "My superiors say I must take the safe. They will accept responsibility and deal with the court, if need be."

"May I have the name or names of your superiors? I'll need them for my article." The pressman was feeling triumphant. Defiantly, the policeman said that he would have to get in touch with the station because the names of such personnel were deemed to be classified. The news reporter suspected that the policeman was lying. In bland tone said, "I might just do that."

As soon as the two men and the safe had left, Sharron sat in the nearest armchair and laughed. She looked at the clock, decided that she'd ring for a pizza delivery and went to the fridge, took out a bottle of red wine and poured out a large measure in the largest glass. What an exciting time!! She pondered over the duel between the reporter and the policeman. So, with feet up and TV on, sipping the wine, waited for the pizza, she tried to imagine the scene at the police station, as they eventually opened the safe. More loud laughter and larger sips of wine. She thought, occasionally heaven gives you one. She couldn't recall from which soap she'd heard that line, but how apt it was just now. Yet, even in her over the top giggly state, a nagging thought still was bothering her. Who was the man with the child that handed over the message giving details about the safe? The only person who knew the combination was Jeff.

Not only that, the child seemed to be telling the man something before he spoke to her. So, this could only mean Jeff was alive. Maybe he was in hiding and the man with the child knows where he is. But why would he be in hiding?!

197

Chapter Fifteen
Multiple Personality

Norman and Maria, eating supper with the TV showing the morning's interview, when the front doorbell rang.

"Okay, I'll get it," said Norman.

"Are you expecting anyone?"

"No, nobody," said Maria without averting her look at the TV.

"Look who it is. This is a surprise. Maria, guess who's here?"

Maria turned to face her cousin, Louis.

Smiling, she said, "How long are you here for? When did you get back? Are you still based in north England?"

"Here for just a week and yes am still stationed in the same place."

"We're just in the middle of supper, care to join us, or have you eaten?"

"I am a bit peckish, so I'll have what you are having."

As Maria left the room to get some food for Louis, the sound of the piano startled Louis.

"Wow, by any chance did you know I was coming? Who is playing the piano?"

"It's Leroy. But I don't understand. What's that got to do with your visit?"

"I'll tell you what. That tune is a folk song in Yorkshire."

With that, he began singing, 'Where hast tha bin since I saw thee, on Ilka Moor Bah Tat, on Ilka Moor Bah tat—on Ilka Moor Bat – on Ilka Moor Tat, on…"

"Hang on, Louis, I don't get it. Is that English or what?"

"It is and it isn't. It's Yorkshire dialect, but more to the point. Who taught Leroy the song? And another thing, he is only three years old."

Louis' tone suggested he was a little on the shocked side.

As Maria entered with his food, Louis said, "Maria, how long has Leroy been studying the piano?"

Maria, answering with a smile, "He only saw and played a keyboard yesterday. My friend and neighbour bought one and as soon as he set it up, Leroy dashed over and started playing."

Louis, still in a state of pure surprise, said, "Okay, I have heard of infant and child prodigies, but where did he hear or know about 'On Ilka Moor?"

For a few moments, there was a puzzled silence and expressions. Norman took the opportunity to say something. "What worries me is the nightmares he has been having. He often shouts out 'Save the children! And 'Jeff where are you, help!"

"Apart from that, is he okay, physically?" Louis said trying to lighten up the atmosphere.

"Has he seen a doctor?"

"We've talked about it. The thing is, now that both Norman and I are working and it is hard to get time off, and as long as there is nothing really wrong with him, we don't see the point."

Louis thought it best not to pursue the matter further. The meal ended, and the conversation turned the usual family matters. So, after an hour or so, Louis went on his way. He said he would try call again before going back to England. After mulling over the evening event, Norman thought maybe it wouldn't be a bad idea for Leroy to see a top psychologist or anyone who is a specialist in the science of the mind. How much would that cost? And where would the dough come from? Although, maybe Top Line TV that asked about the tune Leroy was playing, would want to know more about him. He made a mental note to speak to Maria after work tomorrow. The following day produced another surprise. At the nursery, Leroy spent all the time playing music from the classics, opera, jazz, and even new world. Norman was able to persuade Maria to get in touch with Top Line TV. They did so, and after telling about the circumstances regarding 'Ilka Moor' tune, The TV station felt that Leroy should be interviewed by a psychologist. They would finance the meeting because it would be good publicity for the station which would mean they could increase charges to their sponsors.

So, one week later, Top Line TV interviewed Norman, Maria and Leroy as well as two psychologists. One was convinced that Leroy was a multi-personality child, the other did not accept that there was such a thing as multi personality. A date was arranged but due to a riot, it had to be postponed. When things cooled down, a concert was arranged to raise money for those injured in the riot, be they black or white. It was well attended. After Maria gave her solo performance, she introduced Leroy, saying that she had no idea what he would play. When eventually Leroy sat at the piano, he played Rachmaninov's Etudes.

Although, when he finished and received a standing ovation, it is doubtful that even a handful of the audience recognised what he had played. Top Line TV lost no time in contacting Norman and Maria. They suggested that sometime during the following week, the family should take part in a programme with two psychologists. One, who accepted multi-personality disorder and the other, who opposed the idea. It was only when Norman managed to persuade Maria, that the fee would help the family expenses. With reluctance, Maria finally agreed, but only on condition that there would be no follow-ups. She was adamant that Leroy should live a normal life and not, as she put it, a freak talk show. Her views became entrenched because during the programme, the discussions between the two psychologists became heated. In fact, after Leroy played a few tunes including the Etude he performed the previous week, the psychologists asked him a few questions. They interpreted his answers differently. They both agreed that the best way to clarify the position was, by way of hypnosis. Maria would not hear of it and in a huff, terminated the interviews. Norman tried to placate her and the producers, but did not succeed. The following morning, the local press featured the incident on the front page. The incident would have died a natural death had it not been for what was about to happen the following day. Norman's friend Bert was after a new car. So they went to the local car sales. Maria said it would be good for Leroy to get away from music.

Even though Norman was not in favour, he agreed to take Leroy with them. Bert tried a few models. He finally decided on one. He started the ignition and Leroy shouted, "No good!"

The salesman, Bert and Norman were stunned into silence. Leroy repeated, "No good, cracked cylinder."

Bert was only too aware that used car salesmen were not always fully accurate in describing the state of the goods they were selling. He knew from past experience that there might be trouble ahead if he did not listen to Leroy. So he said, "Let's let your mechanic look at it, even just to stop the kid shouting."

He was smiling as he was speaking and winking at the others. The salesmen, frowning, reluctantly agreed. Also, looking to change his car was a reporter of a local newspaper

201

who overheard what had happened. He recognised Leroy and walked over to Norman.

"You are the father of young Leroy Washington?"

"Yes, that's me. Why do you ask?"

"I saw what just happened and I have my eye on an auto. Would it be okay if Leroy would listen to the engine?"

Norman, ever ready to make a fast buck said, "I'm not sure. It's time we were getting back home for..."

"Tell you what. There's twenty bucks in it for you."

"Make it thirty and I'll ask Leroy if he feels up to it."

The man nodded.

"Leroy, I'd like you to listen to this guy's engine."

Norman took Leroy by the hand, whilst the reporter turned the ignition key. In less than three seconds, Leroy said, "Sounds like a loose cam cover in there."

It turned out, he was correct. The sales manager insisted that Norman and Leroy leave and not come back. Bert looked embarrassed. He said, "If my friend is not welcomed here, then I'll leave and go elsewhere."

The following morning at breakfast, Maria erupted into high volume.

"Norman, what is this all about?"

She threw the newspaper at him. A startled Norman looked up furtively and read 'Yesterday, I was at Grand Auto sales looking for a good used model, when I saw and heard a salesman arguing with another customer. The musical infant prodigy, Leroy Washington heard something wrong with the engine. In short, Norman Washington, Leroy's father was told to leave the premises and not come back. However, before that, I persuaded Mr Washington to allow Leroy to listen to engine of the auto I might have wanted. He listened and there was something wrong.'

"Well, Norman, what have you got to say? How many times do must I tell you I do not want Leroy to be turned into some sort of freak side show? Do I make myself clear?"

No sooner had Maria finished speaking, when the phone rang. It was Top Line TV. Maria took the call. Within seconds, she gave vent to her feelings, saying, "I thought I made myself clear, under no circumstances will I allow my son to be treated as a specimen."

By the tone of her voice and the way she replaced the receiver, Norman felt he was in 'dog house' trouble. He asked feebly, "Who was it and what did they want?"

"It was the TV station. They thought it might be a good idea, as they put it, if I might reconsider Hypnotic investigation for Leroy. All because of the newspaper article. Norman Washington, you are in big trouble. Do you hear me?"

"Oh, come on, Maria. How was I supposed to know that Leroy knew anything about auto engines? Don't forget it was your idea that he should go with me and Bert to the garage."

Maria, glaring at Norman, did not say anything for a short while but finally admitted that Norman was right. Norman took advantage of the long pause that followed.

"I have an idea. Let's call the station and ask them to interview you here, outside. Also, get in touch now with all the women's organisations, well, maybe not all, just those that are interested in childcare and see if they would send a representative to witness the interview and maybe even take part. What do you say?"

Maria agreed. But told Norman he must make the arrangements because she had rehearsals for most of the day. It would be a lot of hassle but Norman thought it was a price worth paying to be out of the dog house.

The following day, with six reps of women's groups and a few newspaper reporters, Maria read her prepared statement.

"Thank you all for coming. In particular, all the ladies from the six groups and their supporters. My message is a simple one. But very important. I believe, as I am sure you do, that all children must have a childhood that allows them to be children in the classic traditional sense of the word. Whether or not they have talents that are above the norm, or not, it is for this reason I refuse to allow my son to be subjected to the so-called 'Hypnotic therapy' in order to find out why he is a child prodigy, so far as his musical talents are concerned. I wish therefore, that the media, be it radio, TV or the press, to cease harassing me about this. Very soon there will be an election for the next president. I know the candidates will be taking notice of my statement. I ask them for their support. Thank you all for listening to me."

By the time Maria finished, a fairly large crowd had gathered. A press reporter shouted out, "Maria! Don't you realise that worldwide, there are hundreds of thousands, if not millions of people, young and old who are suffering with mental disorders and there could be a chance that Leroy may help bring about a cure!?"

To the cheers of some of the crowd, Maria retorted, "And maybe not!"

Soon, those who supported Maria were involved in heated exchanges with those who disagreed. The arguments became more heated and at one point, blows were exchanged. The sound of a police siren reduced the shouting to an angry murmur. A cop stepped out and walked towards the two belligerents.

"Okay, that's enough, break it up folks. The show's over. Move on."

Maria managed to grab a mic.

"This show may be over, but don't forget, I'll be singing at the charity concert tomorrow night, eight o'clock. It is in aid of the victims of the recent riots, both black, like me and white folks. So come along and open your wallets."

The incident would have finished there and then, but the TV reporter stepped in front of Norman and asked, "Mr Washington, do you think Leroy should undergo some hypnotic therapy?"

For Norman, this was an awkward situation. If he agreed with Maria, he would be seen as a 'wimp', if he disagreed, it would be eternal 'Dog house city.'

He answered, tried not to sound too weak., "I know nothing about these matters and when I was growing up we had a saying in our house 'Mother knows best.' I still think that way today."

As the crowed continuing to disperse, the men laughed and the women cheered and clapped.

Later that night, after Norman had finished his late shift and Maria came back after the concert finished, they both flopped on their favourite chairs. They were so tired they couldn't be bothered to switch on the TV. Norman said, "I think a nightcap is in order. What about you?"

"Sure, why not?" Maria answered drowsily, "After all, noise and tension of the morning and the hard work at the concert, I need something to calm me down."

"Me too, but when I said nightcap, that's exactly what I meant. A mug of hot malted milk. What about you?"

"I'll have the same."

Although what she wanted was a shot of rye. After all, if Norman, the drinker, could dumb down to milk, she couldn't take alcohol after all the complaining about the Norman of the old days. Norman made his way into the kitchen and called out, "Sometimes, I do wish Leroy was an average simple kid. It would make life so much better for us, not that I don't love him as he is but..."

"Yeah, I know what you mean. I'm the same. It's not as though there have never been other child prodigies. Especially musicians."

"Okay, here's your drink".

For a short while, they sat in silence. Each, wrapped up in their thoughts. Both wanted to say something but were not sure how to begin. Neither wanted to say anything that might upset the other. Norman, taking a large gulp of the warm comforting warm milk, opened up.

"Did you read the account of this morning's kerfuffle in the evening paper?"

"I did and I am not happy. I see the politicians are using our Leroy as an issue. It's not as though they care about him. All they want is to grab votes for the Presidential election."

"I agree. Did you read what the Independent candidate said?"

"No, was he any better than the others?"

Norman breathed a sigh of relief. "He agrees with you. He said parents' wishes come first. We don't want teacher unions telling us how to educate our kids."

"I'm pleased that at least one politician listens to us." Maria felt better, much to Norman's delight.

"He not only supported us, but went on to say 'we don't want to be like the British where the lefties ignore the wishes of the parents. Their Teachers Unions think they should control how to educate British children with the parents not having a say.'"

By now, Maria was feeling very tired. She looked at the wall clock and said, "Norman, I've had enough for today. I need bed. Maybe in the morning I'll feel calmer. Are you coming?"

"In a short while. I'll watch a little telly first."

"Okay, but don't stay down too long."

The adverts were just finishing as Norman switched on the telly.

"We bring you a News Flash. Both the Presidential Candidates declined to comment on the Independent's statement about the Leroy Washington controversy."

Norman sighed. Switched off the telly and went to bed. There will be trouble ahead.

Chapter Sixteen
Problems for Sid and Simon

It was a bright, sunny Sunday in the Smith household. Fried eggs on toast all round. Tracey, coming in the dining room, stopped short as she heard Simon saying to Sid, "Dad, look at this." He sounded excited. Sid stretched over to look at the Sunday Paper. Tracey slowly made her way back to the kitchen, sat down and poured herself a coffee. This was getting worse. Okay, she knew that Simon was advanced for his age, but reading a Sunday Paper!! As much as she tried to enjoy her egg on toast, it was no use. She decided: once and for all, Sid better explain.

Sid called out, "Tracey, are you coming to have breakfast? We've nearly finished ours."

"Right, a soon as you're done, fetch the plates in here. I must have a word with you."

"Okay, Tracey, what gives?"

"I want to know just what's going on with you and Simon. You always spend a lot of time with him and poor old Lenny gets neglected."

"Come on. In the first-place, Lenny likes to mix in with other children, he enjoys football and other ball games as well. Simon, on the other hand, is more introverted. As you know, he is advanced for his age. He's sooner read a book than play out. I don't know what you are worried about."

"I'm bothered about that he is very strange. Did you know he gave the baby sitter advice on Economics?"

"Look, Tracey, all I can tell you is that Simon is really special. Just accept him for what he is."

"That's the problem. I've no idea what he is and you won't tell me."

"Tracey, just trust me. Simon does not do anything wrong. He hardly does anything wrong. Just be thankful we have two heathy boys who get on well with each other. Leave it at that."

"I'm sorry, Sid. I can't. Friend of mine knows a Medium who may give us some answers. So, I've arranged for her to come here tomorrow night and..."

"No way. I don't go in for hocus pocus and all that weirdo drivel. I absolutely forbid it, Tracey."

"Excuse me. Since when did you become the only one to bring up our children?" Tracey sounded angry and hurt. Sid softened his approach.

"I'm sorry, if I came over harsh. Truth is, I know exactly why Simon is the way he is. But as I said, there is nothing to worry about and there is no need to involve outsiders."

"Really! Then why haven't you told me before. And what's more what makes you think you know?"

"If I told you, you wouldn't believe me. Just trust me. In a few years' time Simon, will just be like any other bright kid. So, no crackpot Spiritualists or Mediums."

Tracey didn't respond. She looked furious and stormed out.

In a few moments, she returned, brandishing the Sunday Paper.

"You'll be surprised to know I was up early this morning and read the article you and Simon were interested in. I noticed there was child Genius in America who can play any musical instrument."

"Well, what's that got to do with Simon?"

"Did you read that there is a debate going on about him having hypnotic investigation and other specialists examining

209

him? Not only that, it could be a political issue in the US Presidential election."

"You mean, Leroy Washington?"

Tracey nodded.

"I can tell you, there is nothing wrong with him."

"Oh really!! What about the nightmares?"

Sid paused awhile, then looked up and in a serious tone, said, "Tracey, Simon knows all the answers. He asked me not to reveal the truth about him and Leroy Washington. I'll ask him to join us, but you must promise to stay calm and not react. Will you do that please?"

"I don't understand. How on earth would Simon..."

"Tracey, please. Listen to Simon and once again, I beg you not to go up the wall. Please stay calm and remember, Simon loves you very much."

After Simon was finally persuaded to explain the position, Tracey felt her mouth and tongue dry up. She looked opened-mouth and felt as though her blood was draining away. Meekly, she asked for a glass of water.

She looked first at Sid, then with tears rolling down, glanced at Simon. It had taken about half-an-hour for all her questions to be answered. She ran out of the kitchen, went upstairs, and packed a suitcase. Sid followed her and asked, "What's all this, Tracey? Where are you going?"

"Not sure. I must get away. I can't take all this. I have to clear my head."

"I've a better idea. Let's go out this evening to the 'Rose and Crown'. We'll have a slap-up meal and have lots to drink. My treat."

Tracey stopped packing and hugged and kissed Sid. "How could any woman refuse such a fantastic offer?"

Meanwhile, Simon, who would in future, be called by his real name Jeff, managed to control his sadness by playing football with Lenny. He was worried by all the fuss going on in Baltimore regarding Martin. If only, somehow, he could tell the world that Leroy was not having nightmares, but recalling events of his past life. If only it were possible for him to speak to the Washington family. This thought kept nagging him through the years he was growing up. He had no difficulty at school, indeed he sailed through the Accountancy and found a place in Willows and Sanford, where he used to work. So why now, three in the afternoon, in his new office, sitting with his feet up and glass of scotch in his hand, was he having such mixed feelings?

Once again, twenty years after the 2016 American Presidential Elections, Leroy Washington, his old pal Martin was once again in the news. What a shock the result of that election had been. It was so devastating, worldwide the financial markets were a mass of confusion. All because, expert opinion was divided. Those who wanted to use hypnosis on Leroy because they were sure it could help advance research into the way the brain works, which could alleviate mental illness. And those who said it would be a waste of time.

The public, too was divided, but most agreed with Maria. The wishes of the mother must come first. The Independent candidate sided with Maria as did all the women's groups. He challenged the Republican and Democrat Candidates to state firmly where they stood on the issue. Both Candidates and their supporters were afraid to do so. On one hand, the wishes of the mother were important, but so was advancement in metal health cures. The result was an overwhelming vote for the independent.

Today, Leroy, hailed as one of the greatest instrumentalists of all time, was having trouble with nightmares, which were in fact, just recalls of his life as Martin. Not just the accident, but times before the accident. He had been hospitalised for observation. This situation marred Jeff's (He now called himself Jeffery Simon) happiness. Because he had exposed the guilty parties regarding the Embezzlement scandal, he had been made a partner.

His thoughts were interrupted by the phone.

"The Clarion on the line for you, Shirley Searcher."
"Okay, put her through. Good afternoon, Shirley."

"Afternoon, Mr Smith. About your message, you say you have the answer to the Brooklyn edge disaster. As you know, other readers have offered their views which you said were all wrong and that only you know the truth. Why should I believe you and not the others?"

"I can't tell you over the phone. All I can say now is, I was there on the bus. If you would care to have dinner with me, my treat, I'll give you full details. By the way, I am a fan of your column."

"Well, I'm not one to pass up a bargain. So, when and where?"

"Do you know the new restaurant, The Magic Lamp?"

"I know where it is, though I've never been."

"I've been a few times. I can promise you a great meal and a fascinating story. In fact, it is so incredible you may be reluctant to print it."

"In that case, I would be wasting my time."

"You'll never know if you don't take up my offer. Either way, you'll get a five-star meal and top class wine. So, you can't lose."

"I must check my diary and call you back."

"Can't wait. Oh, by the way, you'll be in for real surprise."

Chapter Seventeen
Triumph and Tragedy

"Okay Guys and Gals. Any questions or comments? Guy in the third row go ahead."

"I am not happy with the opening chapter. The genre is supposed to be fantasy, maybe sci-fi. Yet, it is not till we get to chapter four is there any mention of the accident. It seems to me that the story is basically Love and Romance with Fantasy as a sub-genre."

The Chairman asked, "Does anyone agree with what has just been said?"

The shouts of 'Yes and No' seemed to cancel each other out. The Chairman continued, "I think we need a show of hands. All those who agree with the criticism raise your hands. Now, those who agree with the author. I think we have a tie. As it's almost lunch time, I'll take one more comment or question. Young lady at the back."

"What's the difference? The book is a best seller."

This brought laughter cheers. The guy in the third row shouted out, "If Chapter four had been first, the book would have sold even more."

Lots of jeers and cries of 'rubbish!' and more shouting followed by the Chairman banging his gavel, "That's it folks. Time to eat."

The events that followed seemed a noisy blur. After lunch, spokesman and women from the Republican and Democrats camps, entered the hall. They insisted that they should ask questions about the book. The Chairman, a quiet man, let them go ahead.

I was surprised when the Democrat asked if I were U.S. citizen who I would consider voting for. I paused for a longish time before answering. I couldn't work out why the politicians came to the workshop. Was my book and reputation so popular that they had to get in on the act? I answered that from what I knew about American politics, I would consider choosing one of the Independent candidates. The applause and cheers were deafening. When it died down, the Republican grabbed the microphone and shouted, "You see, folks, just how low the Demies have sunk. They embarrass a guest in our country in an effort to avoid their impending defeat."

Once more cheers and boos filled the hall.

I was not happy about this intrusion, yet the evening news media gave my book, top billing. So, I did not complain. I would have been happy had not the sad, devastating phone call from my daughter shocked me.

We were back at the hotel. Jo and Jackie were already seated at the lounge bar. Jackie at the far end and Jo about the middle. I sat next to Jo. I was about to order a round of drinks when my mobile came to life. It was my daughter, Sue. My wonderful Sandra had been rushed to hospital, complaining of severe stomach pains. She was dead on arrival. Cause of death, aneurism. My whole world came crashing down. The tears and heavy sobs silenced the other people. Even Jackie walked over to see what had happened. Jo caressed me. I asked Jackie how soon we could return home. The word soon spread and the Republican candidate said he would arrange for one of his company's helicopters to fly me over to Leeds as soon as we landed in Manchester. Not to be outdone, the Democrats drove me and Jo to the airport. Jackie did not go with us. Said she still had work to do. The funeral took place a few days later. The fact that my personal grief proved to be good publicity and that there was a sudden surge in sales, did nothing to alleviate my deep sadness. For a month, I hardly left home. Had it not been for Sue's love and comfort, I would have lapsed in to melancholia. Jo, too, came to visit me, which I greatly appreciated. The hardest part was, I couldn't enjoy my millions with Sandra there to share them.

Gradually, Sue and Jo pulled me round. They persuaded me to spend time writing a sequel to Dilemma and perhaps a story about how I was feeling. With great effort, I managed to do just that. Soon, I hope to have a follow up to Dilemma, and possibly a story based on one of its characters.

THE END

(Sequels to follow)